to Munnar

Anantinee 'JHUMPA' M[illegible]

Invincible Publishers

First Printing: 2019

ISBN: 978-93-89600-11-7

Invincible Publishers

Registered Address: 201A, SAS Tower, Sector 38, Gurgaon - 122003

Manhattan To Munnar is the heart melting story of Veera and Sameera, as they embark on a journey full of love, happiness and a sense of belonging. It is the story of Veera-Sameera and Sid-Rohaan, the two siblings, who form an unbreakable friendship with the two sisters. The heartbreak they experience and the revival from it takes it forward. A story about loyalty, friendship, strength, dilemma, turmoil and mending of a broken heart, from an eleven year old's perspective.

A tale of faith and belief. A tale of the strength of friendship.

Happy reading!!

Gratitude

I thank the Almighty for showering me with strength, skill and passion for writing. I also take this opportunity to thank my Gods in human form: my beloved parents, my MAMA for letting me try my limits and my BABA for encouraging me through them. Many thanks to my grandfather- Gugi Papa for his continuous efforts in making me recognize my abilities and my most affectionate grandmother- Kunimaa for all those helpful and understanding words of inexpressible comfort. I would also take a moment to express my heartfelt gratitude to all my honorable and knowledgeable teachers, my supporting and encouraging family members and loving friends for all their good wishes. My sincere gratitude to the most dynamic team of Invincible Publishers for publishing my books.

- Anantinee 'JHUMPA' Mishra

Prologue

A girl of about sixteen-seventeen, wearing a red polka dot dress was wandering along the hills of Munnar. She had a camera in hand, but her attention was clearly somewhere else. Her eyes were glazed and lost as she searched for something between the valleys of the mountains. It was 6 am in the morning, and not many tourists that came here had such fitness and dedication that they wake up at the crack of the dawn to witness the picturesque scene. As a result, a young boy, Kesar, was surprised to see a pretty girl so early in his father's tea stall. Her cheeks were a pleasant red from the cold and she was rubbing her hands to warm them.

She sat on one of the benches of the stall and turned towards Kesar. 'Hi. One strong tea for me, please.' She said in a slightly shivery voice, and Kesar at once stepped inside their booth to make her required drink. As he boiled water, it struck him that he should strike a conversation with her. '*Didi,* I've never seen you here before. I don't think you are a local. Are you new here?' He asked, looking at her. The girl looked towards him and shook her head. 'I am sorry, I couldn't hear you. Can you please repeat?' She said apologetically. 'I was saying, Didi, that I've never seen you here before. Are you new here?' He asked.

'Oh, no. I am actually a tourist. What about you? This is your stall?' She asked, gesturing toward the stove, ingredient supplies and the few benches. 'Nah. It is Appa's.'

'Appa?' Asked the girl, incredulous. 'My Dad's. Anyway, Didi here is your tea. Careful, it is warm.' He said, handing the paper cup to the girl. They sat in silence for the rest of the time: the girl observing her surroundings and sipping her drink, and Kesar preparing his stove with ingredients for the rush hour which would come later in the morning. The girl didn't look like she wanted to converse any further and Kesar didn't force her.

At last, she had drained her cup and she stood up. 'Here you go.' She handed Kesar a ten-rupee note. As she turned to leave, one last question entered Kesar's mind, yearning to be asked. 'Didi! What is your name?' He shouted after her. The girl's face lost all its warmth. Her back still turned towards Kesar, she closed her eyes shut and went into a flashback.

1

It was an absolutely normal day in the heart of New York, Manhattan. 11th Avenue 42nd Street's houses were silent but at the same time chirping with activity. If we move a bit closer, we will notice a particular apartment, with three occupants, all in its sitting room. If we move close further, we will notice a young girl of around fifteen flipping through her magazine. To be more precise, Veera Maheshwari was flipping a magazine. Her mother was sitting and relaxing, having finally finished all the household chores. Her elder daughter and Veera's elder sister, Sameera, was sitting with Ginger, their pet cat in her lap. She was scratching it behind the ear.

The houses were in eerie silence until a black-haired, tall man entered the room; Veera and Sameera's Dad, Mrs. Maheshwari's husband, Mr. Anant Maheshwari.

'Hi, Dad. How come you are so early from office?' Asked Veera as Sameera carefully put Ginger on the floor and got up to give him a hug. Mr. Maheshwari didn't answer and in one breath said 'Ihavebeentransferredtoindia.' 'What?' Shouted

Mrs. Mahehswari. 'I have been transferred to India.' He scared.

'What?' Mrs. Maheshwari shrieked at the top of her voice for the second time, such that their -pet cat, Ginger, scrambled between Veera's legs and hurried under the sofa. 'We simply can't move like that. Our home, Veera and Sameera's schools and your office! Everything is here. We are settled and happy. No, Anant dear, but we are not ready for this at all. '

'Yes, I know that Akshara dear, but we have to. It is not in my hands. My boss today called for an urgent transfer as the bloke in charge of our Indian assignments in architecture resigned quite unexpectedly. But think about the benefits we would get. Increase in salary, better options in career! Just think! India is known for the quality preliminary education it offers.

Veera and Sameera could have a better future secured. 'Insisted Mr. Maheshwari. 'But Dad, my friends! I cannot imagine living without Sarah, Crystal and Hannah!' Wailed Veera. ' It will take time for you to adjust, I understand. But you cannot always be dependent upon your friends. You have to learn to adjust to new people comfortably. Moreover, you already know a little bit of Hindi. So you would not have any problem with communication.' Soothed Mr. Maheshwari.

'But Anant dear you are missing one very important point, Finances. Packers will take a very high amount of dollars for packing all our stuff at such short notice. Shifting it to India will also be very expensive. If it would have been a matter of shifting within the United States, I would have somewhat agreed. Shifting to another continent would include a lot of tiring and tedious paperwork which includes visa and tickets. It would at least a month for all of that. And I absolutely can't handle that stuff.' Mrs. Maheshwari told her husband very sternly.

But Mr. Maheshwari said, 'No problem there, no problem there! My office has handled everything. Yours, Veera's, Sameera's and my visa and tickets; everything will be handled by them. And no problem in finances as all the financial support, transfer expenditure and costing of tickets will come directly from my company's fund.' Mrs. Maheshwari kept silent for a moment but her requirement was fulfilled by Sameera, Veera's elder sister. 'Dad, can't we just stay here? You aren't the only person in your office, can't someone else go? I don't want any quality education or more money! I am perfectly fine with the way we are.' 'Sameera, darling you have to understand! We have to accept the circumstances! Go upstairs with Veera. Your mother and I shall decide what to do.' Said Mr. Maheshwari exasperatedly. Sameera looked as though she might have argued but grudgingly left for her and Veera's room. Veera followed suit. 'Dad can't do this with us.' Said Sameera as soon as Veera had shut their bedroom door. 'Yeah. This is all his and his office's fault. I mean he also has to follow personal aspects of life as well. He only does that of his professional life.' Agreed Veera. 'What do you say, sis? Should we do something about it?' Said Sameera with an evil grin. And Veera perfectly understood what that grin meant.

Half an hour later Veera and Sameera sat at their dining table, waiting for their lunch. 'Pasta and marmalade.' Said Mrs. Maheshwari handing them two plates. 'Where is Dad?' Asked Veera. Their plan could not be executed without him being present. 'He has gone to the market to get a couple of eggs and bread.' Said Mrs. Maheshwari with pursued lips. Both of them had a shouting match earlier which had made the walls shake. Suddenly, the doorbell rang. 'Sameera, go and open the door. Veera, go to the kitchen, get a plate of pasta and some more marmalade. You will find some in the fridge.'

Both the girls obliged at once, and when Veera returned, she found her sister and father already seated on the dining table. She also sat down, waiting for the signal from Sameera. After what seemed like a century, the signal came. At once Veera scooped her plate and glass, and ignoring the astonished look of her parents, she emptied the entire lot into the bin. Mr. Maheshwari stood up, furious. 'Veera! What a totally ridiculous thing to do! Haven't I and your mother taught you anything regarding not wasting and disrespecting food?' But then…

'Dad! This is my way of displaying that I shall not listen, or pay heed or attention to what you say or do, if you do the same with me. M not leaving America! This is my home. Sameera Di and I…'

'Keep me out of it, Veera! Your plan, my name!' Lied Sameera. She was scared of seeing her father's anger. Rarely, he shouted like this. Frightened, she had chickened out. Though she was feeling very guilty. Shocked, Veera spluttered, 'B…but…y… you…n…no. I… How dare you Sameera?' I devised, 'Enough of this nonsense, Veera! Of all stupid things, this! As your punishment for disrupting the lunch and lying about your sister being involved, no lunch for you today! Go to the garden and trim the flowerbed. I shall come and inspect what you have done. Don't forget to feed Ginger milk and bread crumbs.' Interrupted Mrs. Maheshwari.

Veera stormed into their kitchen, took out some bread crumbs in a plate and milk in a bowl and hurried into their lounge where she found Ginger. Slamming the bowl and plate she placed Ginger in her lap and scratched her behind the ear, while she finished her lunch. 'Nobody understands me, as you do Ginger. Dad doesn't listen to me, mum keeps giving me punishments and Sameera keeps getting me in trouble. But you never disappoint me. Anyway, I'd better get going.'

After completing her chores, Veera went to her and Sameera 's bedroom. She found Sameera sitting on their bed, completing her homework. She did look up as Veera entered. Ignoring Sameera, Veera went inside the washroom to change. When she stepped out, she found Sameera was not in the room. She had just sunk into the cushioned armchair, when Sameera burst inside, carrying a tray. 'Mum has sent bread and cheese with coffee for you.'

'Which I am certainly not going to eat,' Snapped Veera. 'You know what? You are the most insensitive wart I have ever had the misfortune to be related with who doesn't have the guts to defend her sister.'

'I was scared! Scared of witnessing father's anger. I didn't understand what was happening. You don't know how guilty I felt. Forgive me, Veera. I know, I am to blame, but I also know and perhaps hope also that you understand my plight.'

'For your information, I didn't feel scared while emptying my entire lunch in front of mum and Dad!'

'Well, you are courageous.'

'That wasn't courage! That was trust! Trust that you will defend me! Trust that you will not chicken out, or leave me at my situation. It was trust.'

Sameera burst into tears. 'I am sorry! Please!' She shrieked. Veera was shocked to see her in tears. She immediately forgave her and consoled that she was not that seriously angry. Simultaneously they hugged and had just broken apart when their mother's voice echoed from below 'Girls have you finished your snack or should I come and spoon-feed you?' Both Veera and Sameera looked at each other and grinned.

However, their good mood didn't last for long. At dinner that night, Mr. Maheshwari announced, 'I got a call from my office this evening. They informed me that our flight to Delhi will be next week. So the three of you start packing tomorrow onwards. You just pack your clothes and other personal belongings. Furniture and the rest will be packed by the packaging people sent by my office.' Mrs. Maheshwari's ears had turned brick red. Veera and Sameera looked at each other. 'Veera! Sameera! Finish your ham and chicken salad and move upstairs. I shall bring your hot chocolate there.' Shouted Mrs. Maheshwari. Veera waited for Sameera to attack the last spoonful of her dinner and then both of them trotted along the staircase. 'Oh God! What will happen now?' Asked Veera.

"I am totally clueless. Guess will have to wait till tomorrow to find out."

" Yeah, I will see tomorrow.'

'Let us quickly go to sleep or pretend we are sleeping.'

'Seriously? Mum said she would bring hot chocolate.'

'Mum will be in a bad mood. Better not risk it.'

'True. Night,'

'Yeah...Night,'

***

GOING TO VEERA AND SAMEERA 'S SCHOOL AND WITHDRAWING THEIR NAMES. VACATING THE WARDROBES CONTAINING EMERGENCY CASH, PASSWORD DIARIES, JEWELRY, PASSPORTS AND OFFICIAL PAPERWORK (VISA AND TICKETS) AND CITIZENSHIP CERTIFICATES PACKING ANYTHING DELICATE AND NOT FIT TO GO IN THE CARGO GETTING APPROVAL OF VEERA AND SAMEERA'S SCHOOL CHANGING ISSUES; KEEPING THE CERTIFICATE OF APPROVAL, PERCENTAGE RECORDS AND ALL THE CERTIFICATES WON IN SCHOOL IN THE PAPERWORK FOLDER. FLIGHT DETAILS: FLIGHT NO. IC2306, FROM JFK AIRPORT, NEW YORK TO IGI AIRPORT, NEW DELHITIMINGS AND DATE: 11:30 P.M, 27TH OCTOBER 2018. NAMES OF PEOPLE TRAVELLING: Mr. ANANT MAHESHWARI- 39, MALE, Mrs. AKSHARA MAHESHWARI- 38, FEMALE. SAMEERA MAHESHWARI- 17, FEMALE. VEERA MAHESHWARI- 15, FEMALE

'This is the list of things we have to finish by this weekend. After these things are done, I shall inform my transfer department in the office to call the packaging people.' Said Mr. Maheshwari handing the paper to Veera and Sameera. Next morning when they entered the dining room. Mrs. Maheshwari was standing near the stove, cooking their breakfast very ferociously. 'Sameera, go and check the mailbox. Veera, take out eight eggs from the fridge.' She snapped. 'Better do as she says. She looks like an injured lioness.' Said Sameera, hurrying towards the mailbox. After a quiet breakfast which included a lot of glaring daggers and scared looks at each other, Mr. Maheshwari left for office and his wife went to the market.

'Veera, come on. We have some internet surfing to do.'

'Di, seriously? We are going to India and you want to do internet surfing?'

'Yes, sweetheart. We're going to find out the average time it takes from New York to Mumbai.'

'I think, fourteen hours.'

'Via cruise.'

***

'Hmmm. So basically you agree to go to India only under one condition. You want to take a cruise from Southampton to Mumbai. You want to travel by a luxurious vessel The Royal Eureka. How very mature of you.' Said Mr. Maheshwari after presented all the information they had obtained from the internet. They found out a cruise The Royal Eureka which shall leave the ports of Southampton exactly four weeks and three days from today. The tickets were not really that expensive and were going really fast. They figured out that they could take a flight from John F. Kennedy Airport to Southampton Airport.

The Royal Eureka will take about three and a half months to reach the ports of Mumbai. They could again take a flight from Chhatrapati Shivaji Airport of Mumbai to Indira Gandhi Airport of New Delhi. 'We've everything planned. The new academic session starts in India about Four and a half months later and you have to resume your office at the same time. If we would have gone by Airplane then we would have just sat idly for four months and be bored out of our minds. So why not have a little vacation like this?' Said Veera.

'Veera is right, Dad.' Sameera gushed on. 'I agree with Veera and Sameera. We should take this cruise ship, what was its name…yes, the Royal Eureka. I mean we get to relax on such a luxurious ship. And as Veera and Sameera said, it won't do any harm to their academic year as well. Come on Anant, all four of us need this vacation.' Mrs. Maheshwari gave Veera and Sameera a reassuring smile. 'Please, Dad. Please.'

And then…

'OK-OK, I will call my department and tell them to cancel our tickets.' Said Mr. Maheshwari, raising his hands in surrender. 'YAY! We love you Dad, you are the best,' Veera and Sameera shouted simultaneously. And both of them did see him smiling a bit.

2

Four weeks and two days later.

Sameera was sitting on the sofa at the airport when she remembered her last day in Manhattan.

The Maheshwari house was in a turmoil. Everybody was running up and down, hear and there trying to grab anything useful. 'Veera! Sameera! Go to your room and see if you've missed something! I don't want anything last minute tomorrow!' Shouted Mrs. Maheshwari from one floor above.

'OK, Mumma!'

Both the girls left their Vogue Magazines on the table that they had been trying to fit inside their backpacks. They ran upstairs towards their bedroom taking two steps at a time.

'Oh My God! OH MY GOD!' Shouted Sameera as soon as she had closed the door behind her. 'Di! Stop yelling and help me look if we left something.' Said Veera but she too was barely fighting a grin. 'Yup. You see that side.' Sameera's words died in her throat as she looked up to her room. How could she be so ecstatic for a voyage that would take her away from her country, The United States of America? That would take her away from Manhattan? This house held such great memories, she thought. The first time I went to school, the first time I bought my swimming trophy, the time when Veera came home when Veera took her first step, the first time she called her Di. And tomorrow, she would be going away from this place. How could she be happy about it? 'Di what happened?' Said Veera waving her fingers in front of Sameera's face.

'Nothing happened. I…I just zoned out' Said Sameera desperately trying to swallow the lump in her throat. She turned around, so as not to show Veera the wetness in her eyes. One logical part of her body said that this was a reality. She had to accept it, whether today or tomorrow, no matter what. After all, she couldn't run away from reality forever. The other nostalgic half told her that she shouldn't let this happen. She should protest her father's demands. She shouldn't bow down to his unreasonable requests or rather commands.

She again remembered her last day of school.

'Sameera, please don't go! I don't know what I would do without you.' Wailed Safinaa, her childhood best friend. 'I…I am sorry, Safinaa.' Sameera said. 'I am sorry to all of you. Kevin, Joe,

Rosa....everybody. But I can't stay. I have to leave. All I want to say is thank you. Thank you for standing by me no matter what, for always supporting me and being my rock pillar. Thank you so much. I won't say much because I am afraid I will break down.' Tears were now streaming down her pretty face. 'Oh God! C'mon Sameera, group hug.' Rosa and Safinaa enveloped Sameera in a giant bear hug. 'Aren't you both going to say something?' Asked Sameera after she had disentangled herself from Safinaa and Rosa both of whom were now sobbing hysterically. Kevin shook his head. He and Joe too enveloped Sameera into a giant bear hug. 'I'll miss you, Princess.' Whispered Kevin, with the nickname that annoyed Sameera so much.

Sameera gently disentangled herself and ran from there. She didn't stop until she was completely out of breath. 'Hi, Sameera.'

Sameera looked up and saw Tristan Castellan looking upon her, smiling. Tristan had been her childhood crush and a really good friend of hers. 'Hi, Tristan.' She managed to croak. 'Heard you're leaving for India.' There was a sad smile on his face. 'Y...yes. I think Rosa is calling me, Sorry, I need to go.' Sameera wished for nothing more than getting away from him. 'Yeah, I think so, too. Well then,

I wish you a happy and prosperous life, Sameera Maheshwari. I hope we meet again if our fate and destiny allow us to. Good luck to you for your new life. I dare you to ever forget me. Accept it?'

'Tell me, Veera, am I illogical and a coward?' Sameera said, whirling around to face Veera, who was sitting on the armrest of her sofa. 'Yeah,' But upon seeing Sameera's serious face: 'Just kidding. No, you're not even a bit illogical. Why this question right now?'

'Because I don't want to face reality. I don't want to leave Manhattan. I absolutely dread the voyage tomorrow. I want to run away like a coward.' Cried Sameera.

'Di, this is not cowardice at all. You just have anxiety about going to India, making new friends, adjusting to the new lifestyle, that's it! It is scientific human behavior.' Said Veera shaking her sister's shoulders.

Sameera gave Veera a watery smile and playfully ruffled her hair saying 'Since when you become so mature from so childish?' Veera grinned and said 'Time's magic, Di. I know and am confident that everything will go perfectly fine tomorrow.'

Veera had of course no idea how wrong she was.

***

'Wow,' This was the first thing that entered Veera's mind as she saw the luxurious vessel, The Royal Eureka. It was so huge that it reminded her of The Titanic. With a huge entrance deck, with a carved figurehead of a mermaid and an absolutely majestic mast. 'Pinch me, Di,' Said Veera, with her mouth hanging half-open. Sameera obliged and pinched Veera so hard that she yelped and stumbled backward, promptly crashing into someone. 'Whoa! Be careful,' Said the person steadying her shoulders. Veera looked at his face. He had dark brown hair and eyes of even darker brown shade. His hair was messy like he hadn't bothered to brush it up. He was had a fair complexion. He looked about fifteen, of her age. ' Veera! I'm so sorry! Are you all right?' Said Sameera frantically. ' Yeah, Di. I am fine.'

'Ahem,' The boy cleared his throat.

' Yes-yes. Thank you to you ?'

'Siddharth. Sid for short,' Whoa, thought Veera. He is of Indian nationality.

'Thank you, Sid.'

'Girls, are you coming or not?' Mr. and Mrs. Maheshwari had come back after their baggage security check. 'Yes, Mom and Dad.' Veera and Sameera ran towards their parents ,Veera glanced backwards, but the boy had gone.

***

'We've received an invitation to tonight's party. It says that it is a western-themed party, so everybody has to dress accordingly. That means dressing classy.' Said Sameera reading from a golden envelope. Mr. and Mrs. Maheshwari had signed up for a body spa exercise and would be engaged in that all night, so they wouldn't be attending the party.

Both the sisters were in their room. Veera was sipping hot chocolate, while Sameera read out the invitation. They had an absolutely elegant room, which came along with two personalized maids and one butler. It had two separate queen size beds, a TV, a couch, a mini-fridge and a balcony with a personal swimming pool in it. The room was finely carpeted. 'It also says,' Sameera continued, 'It also says that we will get Table No. 4, which we will share with two more people. It sounds like an old classic Hollywood Party. We'll go right?'

Veera shrugged. 'Of course we'll go.' 'Great. Let us go, get our party dresses out.' Said Sameera, standing up. Veera followed suit.

'Veera!!! Are you ready?' Sameera whined. She was really excited to go to the party. She was wearing a black sleeveless knee-length dress. Had put on matching earrings and had let her hair down.

'I'm here, Di.' Said Veera arriving at the door. She looked really pretty, wearing a one-shouldered golden frock, with frills. She had also let her hair down, accessorizing it with short star clips. 'Wow, Di! You're looking absolutely gorgeous!' Exclaimed Veera. 'Less than you, obviously! Shall we go now?' Said Sameera, smiling. Veera nodded and together the two of them left.

The party was a sit-down dinner. As it was a buffet dinner, everybody was bustling here and there. 'That's Table No. 4,' Said Veera, pointing to a table. Both of them moved towards the table. Two people with messy brown hair were sitting there. 'They must be out table mates.' Sameera whispered in Veera's ear. 'Excuse me? We're also...Whoa! Sid!' Veera was surprised as the two of them turned around. 'Hi! Its...?' 'Veera. And this is Sameera, my elder sister.' Said Veera, pointing to Sameera.

'Nice to meet you. I guess I should introduce both the parties as I know both of them.

Veera, Sameera Di, my elder brother Rohaan, Rohaan, Veera and Sameera Di.' Said Sid, pointing to each one of them in the introduction. 'Nice to meet you, Veera and Sameera. Please sit down,' Said Rohaan, smiling. 'Same here,' Said Veera and Sameera together as they sat down. 'So,' Said Sid. 'So?' Asked Sameera. 'Tell us about your life. About the reason you are on the ship.' Said Sid. Veera caught Sameera's eye. 'We don't tell strangers about out life stories, but we will make an exception for two handsome guys', said Veera smiling flirtatiously. 'A long story that is,' Started Veera. 'Well, we had lived in Manhattan since my sister and I were born. Everything was there. Until a few weeks ago when Dad told us that we would be shifting to India on transfer.' Continued Sameera.' It was a shock for both of us. But eventually, we accepted the fact. So now here we are telling you about our life's story.' Finished Veera. 'So I think we have somewhat the same story as yours,' Said Rohaan. 'How?' Asked Sameera.

'Well, both of us lived with our grandma in Southampton. Our parents live in Delhi. Both of us were born in India. I lived with mum and

Dad until Sid was born. At that time, our parents' economic condition was not well, and certainly not well enough to feed themselves and two children three times a day. So they sent us to our Grandma, who was and is quite rich. But now, our parents' condition is stable and off we are, to live with our parents again. Though I must say, I am quite happy to leave our Grandma.' Said Rohaan. When Veera raised her eyebrows, Sid quickly said 'She was a snobby and arrogant lady. Used to make us do things we shouldn't and gives us emotional pressure and mental trauma. We didn't understand what was happening at first, but as we grew older, we learned it was abuse. So when we threatened to go to the police, she stopped it.'

Veera was about to say something when one of the waiters arrived at their table. 'You want me to take your orders, Sirs and Madams?' He asked pointedly. The four of them looked at each other and shook their heads. They decided to go in pairs, Sid and Veera went first to get their food. 'So, Sid, you are traveling alone? I mean just you and Rohaan?' Asked Veera as she piled chicken sausages on her plate. 'Yup. What 'bout you?' Said Sid. 'Well, I'm with Sameera Di, my mum and my Dad.'

'Oh, I see. Umm.. Ok so , what do you want to become when you grow up?' Sid asked curiously. 'Me? Well, I want to become an architect. You know, I always had a strangely queer attraction towards building something permanent.' Shrugged Veera. 'What about you?' 'I want to be a rock star. You know kinda pop star.' Said Sid. 'Cool,' Said Veera 'You know, I think if you put one more item on your plate, it will cause an Earthquake on it,' Laughed Veera, pointing to Sid's plate. He had been absentmindedly loading his plate with servings equal to triple of what he could eat.

'Oh God! I'm the world's biggest and stupidest idiot, even bigger then Bro and that's scying a lot' Said Sid, half amused half horrified. Veera continued to laugh while he scooped the extra food into the trash can. 'Ready to go back to our table?' Asked Veera as soon as Sid straightened up. He nodded, and together they went back to their table, where Rohaan and Sameera were chatting. Veera gestured Rohaan and Sameera to go and get their food. Both of them stood up and moved towards the buffet table while Veera and Sid sat down. 'You know, your size doesn't indicate that you eat this much of food,' Said Veera, gesturing to the mountain of food on Sid's plate that he was ravenously was munching on. 'Aa il tae tat ae compemen.' Sid's mouth was so full that Veera thought it was quite a feat to make any sound at all. He gave an enormous swallow and smiled 'I will take that as a compliment.'

Veera shook her head, and muttered something which sounded like 'Glutton,'. Now smiling slightly, she proceeded to eat. When Sameera and Rohaan returned, she found out that Rohaan fell in the same category as Sid in matters of food. Behind Rohaan, Sameera was suppressing her giggles, gesturing Rohaan's food to Veera. 'You can laugh if you want to,' Said Rohaan. Sameera turned scarlet. 'N…No! I mean I am sorry,' Sameera stuttered lamely. 'You know,' started Sid after Rohaan and Sameera had sat down. He seemed to have not witnessed the exchange between both of them. 'You know, there is a tradition that when we make new friends we should find adjectives that describe each one us. But there is a rule: the adjective's starting letter should be the same as our first name's starting alphabet. Why don't we find such adjectives?'

A moment of silence, then…

'Sacred Sameera!'

'Ravishing Rohaan!'

'Valiant Veera!'

'Super Sid!'

They all looked at each other for a second and then burst out laughing. 'You know the most appropriate one was mine. Super Sid,' Said Sid boastingly. 'Better one will be Schizophrenic Sid,' Said Sameera. Veera and Rohaan howled with laughter, while Sid shot back 'Better than Senti Sameera,'. The evening passed with the four of them insulting each other's names and digging into their food. After making plans of meeting Rohaan and Sid the next day, Sameera and Veera walked back towards their room. 'I had a fab dinner tonight, Veera,' Said Sameera. 'Same here. Oh My God, Rohaan and Sid are so funny.' Howled Veera. 'Keep your voice down, you will wake up the people sleeping in other rooms.' Shushed Sameera.

Said Veera, OK Mom rolling her eyes. Together, the two of them entered their room. The next moment found both Sameera and Veera soundly asleep on their respective beds, without bothering to change their party clothing.

3

The girl's eyes flew open. Sid...Rohan, she thought giddily. She heard the tea stall boy calling after her but, she couldn't bring herself to respond. A voice rang but behand her a voice which was gruff. ' Oi..miser come here'. 'Miser', the word that was the last the girl thought as she was script of her feet the memories the word held...,,

Sameera and Veera had been eating doughnuts in their room the next morning when it happened. The ship gave such a violent jerk that the plate of doughnuts slipped from their coffee table and fell into the floor with a loud CRASH! Veera, who had been holding a cold coffee mug, stumbled and spilled half of it on her shirt. She grasped Sameera 's shoulders for support and after thirty seconds or so, the jerking stopped. Veera released Sameera 's shoulders and shouted 'What the heck was that?' 'No idea. You OK?' Said Sameera, looking at her sister's shirt.

'OK, Mom,' She was soaked with coffee. 'If you call being soaked with coffee OK, then I'm grand.' Snapped Veera. Sameera frowned and said 'Thank God it was cold coffee if it would have been tea or something then...you know what I mean.' Then gesturing to the mess of doughnuts and broken pieces of glass on the floor, she said 'Go, change your shirt. I'll call somebody to clean this.' Veera, while carefully avoiding the pieces of glass, trudged towards the closet, took out a new shirt and headed towards the bathroom to change.

Half an hour later, both Sameera and Veera made their way towards the open deck where they had arranged to meet Sid and Rohaan the previous night. It was a sunny day. The sun was shining brightly and there was a light breeze in the air. Some eight to nine-year-olds were playing on the lower deck, where there was a big swimming pool. They found Sid and Rohaan standing near the railing. Sid waved to them and they made their way towards him. 'Hey, Sid. Hey, Rohaan.' Said Veera and Sameera together. Sid gave them a cheery hello, while Rohaan merely grunted. 'Why the long face?' Sameera asked Rohaan as Veera leaned onto the railing. Before Rohaan could reply to Sameera's question (though he looked like he didn't wish to), Sid said, 'Oh, you know today morning there was this violent jerk. Yeah, so what happened was, we had given all our clothes for ironing and laundry. They had just been returned today morning and Rohaan had been holding the entire set. So when this jerk actually happened, I accidentally dropped the coffee pot that I had been holding. It created a mess on the floor and on top of that Rohaan dropped the entire set, on precisely the same spot. All the cleaning went waste. So now we have to pay extra charges for its cleaning and ironing again. So he is pissed off because of that. Miser.' Veera said, 'How sad,' at the same time as Sameera said, 'Pity.' Rohaan looked at both of them strangely. After a moment, the four of them burst out laughing. Veera had tears of laughter in her eyes while Rohaan was bent over, clutching his stomach. Both Sameera and Sid had grasped the railing for support. After what seemed like an eternity, they stopped laughing when Veera wheezed, 'O...Oh My God! St...op! Can't laugh anymore!' All four gasped, panting for breath. 'Where to now?' Asked Rohaan, once the other three's breathing became regular and normal. 'Should we take a tour or something? I mean of the ship?' Asked Sameera. Everybody agreed to this suggestion and they set off, deciding to visit the lounge first. While they descended the grand marble staircase, only one word entered Sameera's mind to describe the view: lavish. A very sophisticatedly dressed man, waiter Sameera supposed, was holding a tray of colorful drinks, with small umbrellas and fancy straws. As soon as he saw them, he came to them and said in a smooth voice, 'Good morning. These are some complimentary drinks offered by the ship. We have pineapple, peach, lemon, strawberry, blueberry and lime flavors.' Rohaan and Sid grabbed the drinks so fast that it almost spilled on the tray. The waiter rolled his eyes while both the girls laughed and took their own drinks.

Holding their drinks, they went to the Visitors Lounge. The lounge was really luxurious, with a classy wooden sideboard, and a couch with pillows painted with photos from different wonders of the world. A few people were sitting there, reading newspapers or magazines. There was a smoking room as well. From what Sameera could gather, men, usually men, came here after dinner and hung out, smoking and drinking. 'Wow!' Shrieked Veera, wrenching Sameera out of her thoughts. 'Look there is a boutique! We can do all our shopping there!' Veera was excitedly pointing to a small store kind of a cabin. Just at the entrance door, a sign read:

Stephanie's Boutique

Parlor

(Fluffy toys, cute merchandise, pinky handbags, make up including blush, eyeliner and lipstick etcetera, party dresses, cool lingerie, we sell it all! Enjoy shopping!)

Both Sid and Rohaan roll their eyes and say 'We're not going to visit a store that sells 'Fluffy toys, cute merchandise and pinky handbags', understand?' To this Veera hotly replies 'First of all, it is not just any store it 'Stephanie's Boutique Parlour'! Secondly, you're coming whether you like it or not!' Saying so, she grabbed Rohaan and Sid's arms and dragged them inSide, ignoring their protests. Sameera was left to shake her head and roll her eyes in amusement, before following the three of them inside. The store was a complete girly-girly kind of store. Big heart-shaped banners hung from the hot pink ceiling, describing the items on sale. Pink confetti jars were kept on tables. Various dresses were perched on hangers, and a lot of middle-aged women were checking them out. Veera was standing near the makeup section, tapping her foot impatiently while Sid and Rohaan were standing on either side of her and looking as though they would rather be miles away from 'Stephanie's Boutique Parlor.'

As soon as Veera saw Sameera she asked, 'Sameera Di! What was taking you so long?'

'I…uh, I…'

'Forget it. We, that includes you Sid and Rohaan, are going to the makeup section first, after that the dress section and then finally the merchandise section.' Instructed Veera. 'Why the Merchandise Section?' Questioned Sid. 'Because I and Sameera have to buy gifts for all our relatives in India. And you know, I think you ought to buy something for your parents as well.' Said Veera, matter-of-factly. Sid shrugged and followed Veera to the makeup section, with Sameera and Rohaan trotting along behind him. 'Can you please give me one matte lip gloss. Color should be pink, preferably hot pink'. said Veera in a smooth voice to the lady-Miranda, by her nametag, who stood behind the makeup counter. Sid faked gagging; Rohaan snorted and looked in another direction; Veera scowled deeply while Sameera burst out laughing.

One and half hours later, the four of them walked out of the shops, Veera carryings tons of shopping bags. 'Veera, your sneakers' laces are open.' Said Sameera, pointing towards Veera's white sneakers. Veera sent Sameera a thumbs up and was bending down to tie her laces, all the while balancing her bags, when…

BAM!

Something or someone crashed into Veera, sending her crashing towards the floor. All the bags flew in the air, with the contents coming crashing into the floor, the same as Veera. 'Oh My God! Are all these middle-class people blind or something? They keep on colliding with normal, decent people and ruining their cheerful mood! Freak!' Said a snobby voice. Veera looked up to see a beautiful girl with princess blonde curls and perfect blue eyes. She was wearing a sleeveless white polo shirt with a short pink mini skirt. She was swaying her hips in a very arrogant manner and was accompanied by two pretty girls.

Even before Veera could react to what the snobby girl had said, Sameera shrieked with outrage and lunged at the girl. Instinctively, the girl moved backward and went behind her two friends, as if they were going to protect her. Rohaan grabbed Sameera to stop her pouncing on the girl. Sid meanwhile helped Veera up, who was glaring murderously towards the girl. 'See! I proved my point, didn't I? See how they are behaving! Uncivilized! Ill-mannered!' Sneered the girl, though there was a note of panic in her voice.

'Listen here! Just because we aren't saying anything and trying to restrain ourselves doesn't mean that we can't! And first of all, you are the person who doesn't have the proper etiquette to speak and also doesn't have enough guts to come in front and speak, Blondie!' snarled Rohaan, while trying to hold back Sameera. The girl fake laughed and said 'Not Blondie, Amanda Chelsea McKenzie, sweetie. Now-now, you know that you don't have to associate yourself with such people. You and I could have lots of fun together.' She winked at Rohaan, scooting closer.

'You know what? You better start running because if you don't, I'm going to beat the s**t out of you,' Growled Sameera, who now looked livid. Anyone who might be passing the boutique must have thought they were crazy teenagers: Rohaan was trying to restrain Sameera from jumping on Amanda, Amanda was smirking all the while standing behind her two friends, Veera was being held back by Sid and numerous shopping bags were lying all around them, joined by makeup materials and various kinds of dresses. Amanda scoffed and turned to leave, swaying her hips. Both her acquaintances followed suit. At once Sameera turned towards Veera started examining her hands, legs and face, looking for possible injuries.

'Seriously, Di! I'm fine. Ouch!' Veera let out a yelp of pain as Sameera accidentally touched her elbow. Sameera looked horrified as she bent down a bit to have a look at her elbow. 'Fine, huh?' She asked crossly, crossing her arms. Veera gulped and raised her hands in surrender saying, 'Guilty, my lord.' Both Rohaan and Sid laughed loudly, even Sameera managed a small smile. They decided to visit the ship's infirmary to get Veera bandaged (despite her protests) and to the dining room later to have lunch.

'Oh My God! A tiring morning, right Di?' Veera asked, plopping herself down on the room's couch. 'Yes, Oh My God, Sid and Rohaan are so funny! My stomach hurts from laughing so hard.' Wheezed Sameera, squeezing her stomach. 'Right! They are absolutely hilarious!' Laughed Veera. 'I think it's time for a short nap,' Declared Sameera with a yawn, plopping herself on one of the twin beds. Veera went to freshen up and by the time she came back, the sounds of soft snores filled the entire room. Shaking her head and smiling slightly, Veera followed suit.

'Hi, girls. How was your day?' greeted Mrs. Maheshwari as she entered Sameera and Veera's room. Both of them had just woken up from their nap and were sitting on their coffee table, sipping cups of hot chocolate. 'Hi, mum! Just woke up from our short nap,' Exclaimed Veera. 'Our day was awesome mum. We went exploring the ship with Rohaan and Sid. You don't know them, right? Well, we were tablemates for yesterday's dinner. We became friends then only. After the exploration, we went to the dining room for eating our lunch.' Rushed Sameera. Mrs. Maheshwari nodded and went on explaining how she and Mr. Maheshwari spent the entire day relaxing on the decks and had breakfast and lunch there itself. After chatting for half an hour or so, Mrs. Maheshwari left.

4

'Di! It's a text from Sid!' Veera tossed the phone to Sameera.

Hi, Veera. I was wondering if you want to hang out in our room for a while. Room 262, Deluxe Suites. Sid :)

'What say? Should we go?' Asked Veera. Sameera shrugged and said 'Sure, why not,'. They made their way towards the deluxe suites.

'Whoa!' Exclaimed Sameera on entering Sid and Rohaan's 'room'. It was a grand suite, with three rooms, a dining table, a kitchen and a chandelier right in the middle of the sitting room. 'Now I get it why these bunch of cabins are known as Deluxe Suites. They look like some Hollywood film star's bedroom!' Said Sameera, amazed. 'You didn't tell us you were rich!' Said Veera accusingly, glaring at Sid and Rohaan, who looked bemused by Sameera and Veera's totally shocking behavior. 'I didn't mention before that we had gone to live with our Grandma before?' Asked Sid incredulously? 'You did, but you didn't mention that she booked you such a cool cabin!' Said Sameera. 'But Sid did mention that Grandma is rich, right? So she became very happy when she found out that we were leaving, not happier than us, obviously and left her account password in our room. We used it to book us this beauty,' Said Rohaan, pointing towards the cabin.

'Remind me to never leave my passwords anywhere near you two,' muttered Sameera. Sid took a bow while Rohaan grinned like a Cheshire cat. 'So,' Said Veera, settling herself on the sofa leisurely. 'So?' Questioned Rohaan, looking at Veera expectantly, as he, Sameera and Sid too settled themselves comfortably. 'So nothing. So what should we talk about?' Said Veera. 'We should talk about how amazingly cool and superb I am.' Boasted Sid and tugged the collar of his shirt. 'You're so full of yourself. Ugh,' Said Veera. 'You don't know half of it, Veera,' Said Rohaan, placing a Pop-Tart fished out from his breast pocket (Veera was sure there were more of them in his other pockets) in his mouth.

'Let's play Truth-Dare,' Suggested Sameera, sitting up straighter. The others agreed and Veera decided to ask Rohaan first. 'Truth or Dare?' Questioned Veera. 'Dare. Truth is for weaklings,' Said Rohaan confidently. Veera smirked and said 'I dare you to pour two sachets of salt in your lemonade and drink it in thirty seconds.' Rohaan visibly paled as Sameera howled with laughter and Sid got up and got two salt sachets for Rohaan. Rohaan emptied them in his drink.

Taking a deep breath, he drank the entire thing. 'Yuck! Salt Lemonade tastes disgusting!' bleated Rohaan. Sameera high-fived Veera as Sid rolled around the couch, shaking with laughter. Rohaan, who had an evil glint in his eyes, turned to Veera and asked 'Truth or Dare, Veera?' 'Dare. Truth is for weaklings,' She said quoting Rohaan. 'I dare you to put two sachets in two drinks apiece and drink them in one minute.' Veera cringed. This time too, both Sameera and Sid burst out laughing at the horrified look on Veera's face. Sameera got up to get the drinks and salt sachets, but Rohaan stopped her and obliged. Sameera sat down and continued laughing with Sid as Veera just sat there, Half amused by how Sid and her sister were behaving and half stunned by Rohaan's dare to revenge her.

Rohaan returned, holding a tray with two Pineapple juices, four sachets of salt and a spoon. He kept the tray on the table and mixed the sachets in them. He then handed one glass to Veera, smiling sweetly. Veera gulped and took the glass, as Rohaan adjusted his watch. In about twenty seconds, Veera, now green, had finished her first glass and holding her hand to get the second glass. Rohaan, who was trying to cover the fits of laughter so that the glass he was now holding to Veera didn't end up on the floor, but failing miserably. After thirty seconds, Veera kept the glass on the table, panting heavily and clutching her stomach. 'Jesus! I don't believe you made me do that, Rohaan!' Gasped Veera. 'And you two! Stop laughing your heads off!' She added, glaring in Sid and Sameera's direction. Sameera raised her hands in surrender, all the while giggling as Sid rolled around the couch shaking with mirth.

Veera humped and crossed her arms around her chest with a frown on her face. After a few minutes, they resumed the game. 'OK, Sid, Truth or Dare?' Asked Veera. 'Um, truth. I don't trust your dares.' Answered Sid. 'Ha-Ha. Did you have any soft toy when you were little that you used to cuddle or sleep with?' Asked Veera, grinning. Sid turned Tomato red and said quietly 'I did. I still have him. His name is Mr. Bartholomew McDonald.' Everyone was silent for a moment and then Veera, Rohaan and Sameera burst out laughing. 'Mr. Bartholomew McDonald?' Wheezed Sameera between breaths. 'How come I didn't know about him?' Questioned Rohaan, his voice hoarse because of all the laughing. 'I kept it as a secret in my wardrobe, so that you wouldn't find it,' Whispered Sid embarrassedly. 'OK enough laughing, guys. Sameera Di, Truth or Dare?"

Questioned Sid, smiling wickedly. 'Guess I'll go with Dare,' Said Sameera boldly. 'I dare you to spill an entire bottle of coconut water on Veera,' Said Sid with fits of laughter.

Veera indignantly said 'Hey! Not fair!' at the same time as Sameera grinned 'Nice one, Sid! Thanks!'. Veera made a grumpy face as Sid asked Rohaan to get a bottle of Coconut water from the drinks basket and he eagerly obliged. Just as Sameera was about to pour coconut water on Veera's head, the latter shouted 'Wait! If you pour Coconut Water on my head, then my clothes would be ruined and my hair would be sticky. It takes me about an hour to wash my hair. So our game would be disrupted until then as I am sure there would be no fun in playing without me. So I suggest you please change your dare.' 'You know she is correct,' Said Rohaan logically. 'But you can't change it! A dare means you have to do it! Even if it dirties someone's damn hair! If you don't have the guts, then you should not have taken dare in the first place!' Shouted Sid. The room went extremely quiet. Sameera and Rohaan were looking at Veera fearfully. 'You know what?' Started Veera, her voice dangerously calm. 'I do care about my 'damn hair' and if you don't then I don't care. And the next time think twice before you open that big fat mouth of yours, which either opens to praise you stupidity or criticize others' logical thinking.' And the next moment she was out of the door.

Veera sat on her bed, fuming. Who was that Siddharth to teach her whether she should take Truth or Dare? She thought. And the fact that he said that she didn't have enough guts to take dare hurt. A lot. But even more than that, the fact that Sameera or even Rohaan didn't stop her while she was leaving. Maybe, they too think that I'm a drama queen, thought Veera bitterly. But then you are one, aren't you? Questioned one part of her brain. Of course not, thought another one.

'God! I think I should go to sleep now. Not thinking anything right now would definitely do me loads of good.' Muttered Veera. She got up and opened the door's lock (Incase Sameera Di comes back and I'm asleep. I'm a heavy sleeper, thought Veera). She then fell flat on her back, but surprisingly, even though her eyelids felt heavy, she couldn't get any sleep. Random thoughts kept coming to her mind like her best friend Crystal, and her class fifth class teacher Miss Sally etcetera, etcetera. But ultimately, her thoughts kept coming back to what must be Sameera Di and Rohaan thinking about me. She did feel one ounce of guilt at the thought of Siddharth, though. She still couldn't understand why she was referring to him as Siddharth and not Sid.

Probably as they were not on talking terms (as of now, one part of her brain hoped). She checked her phone which was lying on the bed side table. There were no 'I'm sorry' messages from Siddharth nor any 'How're you' messages from Sameera. She kept her phone back on the table, switching it off. She then turned to her Side, punching the pillow to more comfortable position. Maybe, going to sleep is the best and only option for me that is available now, was Veera's last thought before she fell asleep.

Veera woke up next morning to a pillow hitting her face and a familiar voice saying "Wake up, sleepyhead!" Veera groaned and slanted her eyes open. Sameera was standing near the foot of her bed, holding a plate full of muffins and a cup of hot steaming coffee. "Enjoyed gossiping about me yesterday with Rohaan and Siddharth, did you? You look quite fresh today." Growled Veera as soon as the memories of the previous night came rushing back to her. Sameera sighed and said 'I didn't gossip about you, Veera. It took us a lot of time to make Sid realize that he was the one at fault,' 'Yeah? Well then the fact that it took you hours to convince him of guiltiness strengthens my resolution that he is not only an idiot, but also a stubborn, attention-seeking boy!' Shouted Veera.

'Don't make a habit of turning smaller arguments to bigger ones, Veera! You are behaving like an immature two year old! You're behaving like a failure in sisterhood and friendship!' Shouted back Sameera, equally angry. Veera looked down for one minute, not of embarrassment, but trying to regain her composure. She then looked right at Sameera, smiling widely, knowing it would infuriate her. 'Well, the apple doesn't fall far from the tree, does it? You are failure as a sister, I was bound to be one as a sister and friend.' She said calmly. She then got up from the bed, threw the sheets on the floor and walked towards the bathroom, not giving an ear to Sameera's angry screams behind her. She bolted the bathroom's door close and sat down on the edge of the bathtub, breathing and thinking hard. One part of her felt guilty. Guilty that she had shouted on her beloved Sameera Di, guilty that she had behaved immaturely during her fight with Siddharth yesterday, guilty that she had too much of an ego to just go and apologize to Sid. The other part of her felt angry.

Angry on Sameera Di for calling her a failure, angry on Sid for making such a big deal out of nothing and lastly angry on herself for thinking that she was egoistic and a drama queen, because she was not! For once, Veera just wanted to break down into tears and cry until she couldn't anymore. But she couldn't let herself break down because Veera Maheshwari didn't cry for small things or worthless (by that she meant, Siddharth not Sameera Di) people. Nor did she depend on people to make her happy or sad. She was strong, bold and independent, not a weakling. With that, she stood up, determined not to let Siddharth's words take the worst out in her. She wouldn't let Siddharth be proved right, that she was a weakling and didn't have enough guts. She wiped a few tears that had gathered in her eyes. But before Siddharth finally realized his mistake, how many more glares and tantrums she would have to endure from Sameera and possibly Rohaan, she didn't know.

5

Veera got a full blast of cool air as she entered the upper deck of the ship. Not many people were there, just two or three women who were conversing in low tones. She walked towards the rail and leaned across it. The vast blue ocean was spread like a blue blanket, with all the tiny marine organisms in it as patterns. Dolphins kept coming up to the surface to inhale the pure air as the ship jostled forward, cutting its way. 'Hi, Veera.' Came a voice behind her. She whirled around to find Rohaan standing there casually, with hands in his pant pockets and a sad smile on his face. 'Come to find out if little Veera is crying her eyes out or not, have you?" She spat. Rohaan sighed and said 'Sameera told me what happened earlier.'

'All been talking about me, huh? Don't worry, I'm getting used to it.'

'Veera! We wanted to talk to you!'

'Then why didn't you? You preferred to talk to Siddharth first, even though he was the guilty one!'

'That is the reason we talked to Sid first! Because he was the guilty one! There is absolutely no point in explaining things to the right person! The wrong one needs to understand and that's why we decided that Sid's need of understanding was greater than your need of comfort!' At this, Veera stopped. What Rohaan said was actually making sense. Siddharth was the wrong one, not her! So the understanding should go to him only not her! 'I see that you are starting to understand why did we not come to you and stayed with Sid,' Said Rohaan, with a hint of smile on his face. 'Maybe,' Said Veera, smiling slightly. 'Huzzah! Finally Ms. Veera understood the entire scenario. It is a historic day!' Exclaimed Rohaan, punching his fists into the air. Veera let out a hearty laugh, and together, the two of them trudged towards the breakfast area.

The 'Solution talk on the deck' (put forth by Sameera) had some good effects. Best of all was that Sid and Veera were friends again. The latter and Sameera also spent the entire breakfast apologizing to each other and blaming themselves for the entire argument. Sid just sat there bemused by how women change track so fast while Rohaan was simply amused to see both the girls fret over themselves.

Suddenly a man, dressed in a white naval uniform, came there and his voice boomed through the microphone that he was holding.

'Ladies and Gentlemen, boys and girls. We regret to inform a three hour delay, due to a technical mishap which has taken place in the engines. We would be docking in the port in about half an hour. I personally suggest everybody to go out and enjoy the port as it's a very sunny, this morning is, and that is prominently rare. I would insure that tour guides are available at maximum. Then again, any inconvenience caused is deeply regretted.'

Immediately chatters broke out. Some people looked really pissed off while others looked happy that they got to spend an entire day without seasickness and rocking back and forth on the International Atlantic waters. 'What say? Should we go to explore or stay aboard only?' Questioned Veera as she looked around the breakfast hall. 'Nihing e aine,' Said Sid through a mouth full of scrambled eggs and toast. 'You disgust me,' Said Veera, swatting Sid's arm. Sid shrugged and said 'What I said is, 'anything is fine'. Veera shook her head and looked at Sameera and Rohaan for their opinions. 'I think we should go and explore the port.

Anybody knows what is the port's name?' Said Sameera. 'I absolutely don't. My geography and General Awareness is absolutely terrible.' Said Sid with a fake yawn. Sameera rolled her eyes towards

Veera in such a way, as if to say 'Ugh, Boys! I don't know what made me ask this glutton!' 'I say, let's go to the port for a while. If we like it there, then we shall stay longer. If not, then we will come back and goof around the ship for the rest of day. Sounds good?' Said Rohaan sensibly. 'Sounds good,' Confirmed Veera with a nod, after sharing another eye lock with her elder sister. 'Let us meet in the port in about half an hour.'

By the 'port', the crew member meant a large wooden surface, slightly above the altitude. Clean blue water whished and whooshed around the surface, occasionally bringing two three fishes with it. Through the port was connected a huge ground sort of area. A huge fair had been set up there, exclusively for the people of the ship. Cruisers were bustling here and there, some were buying merchandise sold in the tent shops and others were trying out the variety of games specially set up.

'Wow! Let us quickly go and check ot the shops!' Cooed Veera. 'No, absolutely not. We are not spending an entire morning in shops.' Said Sid, shaking his head. 'And why is that?' Said Veera with a frown and crossed her arms so stiffly, as if she is was not going to unravel them for years. 'Because I am sure we will go as quickly as possible but will come as late and delayed as possible'. Said Sid in a matter-of-fact voice. 'I say we split up. How about I and Sid go to check out the games and you and Veera go to check out the shops?' Said Sameera, grinning wickedly at Rohaan. He looked flabbergasted at the thought itself. 'Yeah that is a good idea. Come on Sameera,' Said Sid, giving her a high five such that Rohaan could see the gesture but Veera couldn't.

Rohaan started to say something but Veera had already started marching towards the shops. He gave Sid and Sameera one last murderous look before slouching off behind Veera. 'Good one, Sameera'! Chuckled Sid after both of them had a hearty laugh. 'Yeah, I know! Did you see the look on his face when he realized the splitting plan! Hilarious! Absolutely hilarious!' Said Sameera, grinning from ear to ear. It were simple, carefree and funny moments with friends and family that Sameera always craved for, from her earliest memory. Moments without any complications or expectations. She always had this fear; phobia of failing.

Before trying out something new, the question 'What if I fail?' haunted her night and day. She did fear failure but she feared people's ridicule and criticism even more than that. 'Hellooooo! Back to Earth!' Said Sid, snapping his fingers in front of her face. Sameera flinched and quickly said 'Sorry, I just zoned out.' 'Fine. Come on, race you to Shop No. 2,' Shouted Sid and started running even before Sameera could approve (not that she wasn't going to; she never ran away from a challenge). She just ran after him, shrieking 'Cheater! Cheater!' 'Everything is fair in love and war, Sameera!' He called out behind. Sameera too gave in to a grudging smile.

'Oh God, I am so exhausted!' Moaned Veera as she plopped herself on the sofa of her and Sameera's room. Rohaan too settled himself on the bed, looking at the snacks kept on the table longingly. 'So what did you guys do?' Enquired Sameera. She and Sid had returned back early to explore the ship. They had asked Veera and Rohaan if they would like to go back also, but Veera had refused straight away and Rohaan had no option but to do the same. 'As usual, Veera went crazy at the shops.' Snorted Rohaan. 'Awwww, Bad boy Rohaan had to shop with shopping freak Veera! Sad, man, really sad!' Joked Sid as Sameera burst out laughing and Veera scowled towards the pair of them.

'I am not a shopping freak! I just...'

'Am totally insane about it' Said Sid at the same time Sameera said 'Can't control myself after seeing a shop'. The four of them looked at each other for a split second before again starting to laugh. 'Oh God, I just cannot go to the dining hall to eat! Can we order something?' Said Sameera, as she stretched herself on Veera's bed. 'How do Chicken Burritos and Salad sound?' Said Rohaan, snatching up the menu from the bedside cabinet and surveying it rapidly. 'Mouthwatering' answered Sid with moan. Sameera and Veera also agreed and Rohaan called up the restaurant using the room's landline, ordering their Chicken Burritos. 'I am going to go to freshen up and change into my pajamas. You are coming, Sid?' said Rohaan standing up. Sid followed his brother, and the Maheshwari girls were left to themselves.

After a dinner full of laughter and the sound of teeth chomping or wolfing down Chicken Burritos, Rohaan lay on Sameera's bed, moaning as he rubbed his stomach. 'God, I ate too much today. Three Chicken Burritos! Can you imagine that?' He said. 'Nope. You should have taken one like the non-gluttons that I and Sameera Di are.' Said Veera. 'You have a weak belly, Bro. I ate four and look at me!' Said Sid, doing a very Sid like version of belly dance. Veera picked up a cushion from the couch and threw at him. 'You will make the protocol of belly dance commit suicide!' She said. Sameera chuckled, and Rohaan too, despite his stomach ache, managed a smile.

6

Several weeks had passed away since Veera and Sameera had met Rohaan and Sid. They now spent almost every day together, except for when Veera and Sameera decide to spend the same with their parents. Currently they were gathered in Sid and Rohaan's deluxe suite (Veera preferred to hang put there only as she loved the Mango smoothie that their Sid and Rohaan's butler Matt served). Veera was sitting on the couch, reading a book and sipping Mango smoothie, as Sameera and Rohaan played Chess. Sid was glued to his phone, playing Clash of Clans.

'You know, there is no point in gathering together if everyone is busy doing something or the other individually.' Said Veera, closing her book with a snap and keeping it on the table. 'Hmm?' Said Sid, thoroughly engrossed in his video game. Sameera and Rohaan were still playing chess intently. Veera shook her head, frustrated, and drained her smoothie glass in one and got up to get another one from the fridge. 'I think my little sister is right, let us call it quits,' Said Sameera, leaning back in her chair and rubbing her eyes warily. 'You want to call it quits just because you are losing!' Said Rohaan accusingly at the same time as Veera scowled and said 'I am your sister, not your little sister'.

Sameera just snickered at Rohaan, ignoring Veera's jibe, and slapped all the pawns and chess knights away. They all fell onto the floor, with a series of tip-top sounds. 'Hey!' Shouted Rohaan looking thoroughly aghast. Sid finally looked up from his phone, and seeing the knights and pawns on the floor to Sameera's smirking face to Rohaan's indignant expression to Veera trying to cover up her laughter while getting her smoothie, burst out laughing. Rohaan huffed and crossed his arms indignantly. Just then, Sameera's phone buzzed. 'It is a text from Mumma, Veera!' Said Sameera. 'Read it!' Came Veera's reply. 'Hi, Sameera. 'Was wondering if you girls want to join me and Dad for lunch in about fifteen minutes? If yes, then meet us in Rogue's Rearing Café on the lower deck. If not, do inform me where you guys will be eating. Say hello to Sid and Rohaan from me. Mum.' 'Well then we should get going,' Said Veera, looking sorrowfully at her unfinished smoothie. Sid noticed this ad decided to tease her a bit. 'Don't worry,' Started Sid in mock consolation. 'I will finish the smoothie. It will not go waste.' Veera smacked him on his arm scathingly and marched out of the door with Sameera at her heels.

What the Royal Eureka and people aboard it didn't know was that it was probably the last daylight it would ever see.

It was around midnight. Surprisingly, the entire three decks were empty. There was not a soul in sight. Veera was frantically walking towards the railing. She felt panicky; she could not find her mom, or Dad, or Sameera, or Sid or even Rohaan anywhere. Even the slightest rustle in her surroundings would make her jump about a foot.

Please, she thought desperately, please someone come in view.....I can't tolerate this type of isolation.....Where the heck are you, Sameera Di?

It was then only that she spotted Sameera; she was standing a few feet from her....she was holding out her hand....smiling warmly. Veera was about to take her hand and murder her for making her so terrified.

A high wave arose behind Sameera, so high that it might have been even higher than ten people standing on top each other.

Veera opened her mouth to scream, to warn Sameera, but no sound came out. Sameera shook her head, and when she looked up, there was a sad and painful smile on her face. 'You can't do anything about it, Veera. I have to go away. It is my destiny. I love you.' She said softly. Then spreading her arms wide, she was lifted up in the air, a blinding flash of light, and there was no Sameera. Then everything turned black.

'Veera! Wake up! Veera!'

Veera opened her eyes and found Sameera's worried face hovering above her. Relief, strong relief washed over her. She felt lightheaded like someone had dumped a bucket of ice-cold water above her head. She sat straight and hugged Sameera as tightly as she could. 'Whoa! Veera, what happened? Was it a bad dream? You were screaming your head off!' She said frantically. Only then Veera realized what condition she was in. She was covered in sweat and all the sheets and blankets had been tangled around her legs. Her hands were shaking and her heart was beating in her throat.

'Yeah, a really bad one. No one was on the ship. I was all alone, but then I found you. But then a high wave rose and took you away with it. You said that going away was your destiny. Then everything went black.' Said Veera, trying very hard not to make her voice shake. 'Oh. But it was only a dream Veera, nothing else. Don't think about it. It will be fine, I promise.' Said Sameera coaxingly. Veera nodded and looked at the table clock, five in the evening. 'I am fine, now. Can you make me a cup of strong tea?' She asked Sameera. The latter nodded and squeezed her shoulder in an affectionate sort of way. It was a dream; only a dream, thought Veera, trying to regain her composure. But she couldn't shake off the intuition that something bad was going to happen. Something very bad.

She thought about that fateful day. How everyone had been so clueless about a huge storm that was going to hit their lives. How clueless had she been; but surely more than the Captain and Crew of the ship. When she thought about it later, maybe they might have such a conversation after losing one of their best employees. But whether it was just a figment of her imagination or she was accurate at reading the Captain's mind, no one could ever know now. It was lost in history.........

Captain Jos Peterson was a man with a cool attitude. He was known among the crew for maintaining his sanity in the toughest of decisions. He had currently been sitting in his office, sipping lemon tea and looking a photo of his wife, Mrs. Andrea Peterson, when Mr. Krishnamurthy came bursting in. The captain blinked, taken aback by the sudden appearance of the black-haired man.

'Disaster in the engines. The propeller is not working properly.' He panted, trying to catch his breath. Captain Peterson put his tea and photo on his desk and stood up. 'Did you tell Cedric about this?' He inquired. Cedric Rodriguez was the head mechanical engineer of the ship. 'Yeah, I sent Lucas to go and fetch him,' replied Mr. Krishnamurthy. The captain visibly relaxed, because he knew any kind of mechanical problem and Cedric would be able to solve it in minutes. 'Let us go to the engines. I did want to have a talk with Cedric regarding the speed of the vessel anyway.' Said Captain Peterson. Mr. Krishnamurthy nodded and the two men made their way towards the engines.

The engines were a place full of smoke, fire and soot-covered coal mining people. Just as the Captain had greeted Mr. Mathieu, the head supervisor of the engines, his assistant Lucas came running. He seemed very white and pale. 'Sire! Pray for ze departed soul 'cause Cedric Rodriguez eesn't alive anymore! 'E 'anged heemself!' He gasped. 'Jesus!' Breathed Mathieu. 'HOLY S**T!' Shouted Mr. Krishnamurthy. The Captain who seemed to have frozen from shock, quickly snapped out of his reverie. He seemed to regain his composure and said 'Shh! Someone might hear you!'

However, all the people near them were completely preoccupied with their work and Mr. Krishnamurthy's outburst went unnoticed. He looked around to make sure all the workers were immersed in their work before speaking. 'Krishnamurthy,' He started, addressing Mr. Krishnamurthy. 'Will it be alright if the four of us—Lucas, Mathieu, you and I go to your office to discuss the...ah, situation?' His tone made it clear that he really was not asking for permission. Krishnamurthy nodded, looking scared. The Captain then turned to Lucas. 'Did anyone other than you see the body?' He asked sharply. Lucas shook his head. 'Did you lock the door properly or did you leave it ajar?' He continued. Lucas shook his head again and muttered in a quiet, hoarse voice 'Closed ze door,' Captain Peterson nodded and motioned the other three men to accompany him to Krishnamurthy's office.

'I can't believe this. Today only Rodriguez had to commit suicide of all days!' Said Mathieu burying his face in his hands, as soon as the four of them had settled themselves in Krishnamurthy's office.

'Yes, but we should not dwell or lament on the past when we have a visibly problematic future,' Said the Captain, pacing around the room.

'What are you talking about, Mister Peterson? I didn't understand the statement,' Said Lucas, looking very pale, white and bemused all at once.

'Well, the thing is, we have to hide the fact that Cedric Rodriguez is no more. It will create fear and suspicion among the passengers. Our shipping company is massively depending on this passenger cruise line for placing it in profit and high value in the commercial market.' Said the Captain.

'But how do we explain his absence from the board meetings, and when the propeller is fixed by another mechanical engineer, what will we say that why was Rodreeguez not able to fix it?' Said Mathieu.

'We will think of answers later. But for now, the most important work is disposing Cedric Rodriguez's body. If any room cleaning service finds it, then....you know what will happen.' Said the Captain gravely.

'What I don't understand is,' Mr. Krishnamurthy started slowly, 'Why did Rodriguez commit suicide in the first place. As far as I know, he was a jolly man. And the last I saw him, yesterday evening, he looked quite...normal.'

'I am afraid that the answer to that question can never be found again,' Said Mathieu thoughtfully.

Lucas clasped his hands and said 'So, shall we do ze deesposal now only?'

Everybody looked at the Captain. He shook his head and said, 'No, I don't think so. There are crowds here and there. It would be thoroughly difficult to do it.'

Everybody present in the room knew what did the Captain mean when he said 'it'.

'So how do we do it?' Asked Mr. Krishnamurthy quietly.

'I say we just don't. I don't know, dump him?' Said Mathieu.

The Captain had just opened his mouth to say something when a shrill alarm sound rang out. 'Oh my,' Said Lucas, standing up. Mathieu and Mr. Krishnamurthy shared an eye lock, and the next moment both of them were out of the door, with the latter telling the Captain to meet them in the Emergency Hall within half an hour. Lucas too greeted the Captain and left the room hurriedly. Captain Fredrick Peterson seemed to have frozen with shock. This was the second time he had heard this bell and the first he had heard it…he didn't want to remember that day. He prayed to any God that came to his mind and left the room.

Because he knew that the bell was only to be used in the most emergent of situations. That the bell only meant two things. Trouble. Deadly Trouble. And....death.

7

'Here you go, Veera. Your tea,' Said Sameera, holding out a mug to Veera. 'Thanks, Di.' Said Veera, giving Sameera a small smile. She raised the mug to her lips, tasting the warm liquid. It was with the right amount of sugar and milk, just as Veera liked it. 'Do you want me to call Sid and Rohaan over? Having them joke around can help you cheer up,' said Sameera, trying not to look too worried about Veera.

Veera took another small sip of her hot beverage, and said 'That would be OK.'

Fifteen minutes later Sid and Rohaan had gathered in Veera and Sameera's room, after receiving a call from Sameera.

'...then everything blacked out, and I heard Di's voice, asking me to wake up.' Veera finished recounting her dream to both the boys and leaned back in the bed, taking a deep breath.

'Whoa, Veera! You are pretty creative and imaginative when it comes to dreams!' Said Rohaan, looking amazed. 'What the heck do you mean by that?' Snapped Veera. 'What I mean is, you have quite a unique idea of murdering your own sister.'

Chortled Rohaan. He was, however, spared by Veera's merciless tickling as a punishment when a shrill sound of the bell rang out through the vessel.

'What was that?' Muttered Veera, momentarily forgetting about Rohaan's punishment. 'Dunno. Maybe some sort of bell to....alert the crew or something.' Sid said. 'Alert the crew...of what?' Asked Sameera. Rohaan wasn't saying anything that might remind Veera that she was supposed to be tickling him right now. 'Maybe, some sort of huge and ferocious sea monster?' Laughed Sid. 'I am only joking...joking!' He added, noticing Veera's pale and whitish look. 'Hey! Veera, you need to complete Rohaan's punishment! Forget about this alarm bell stuff!' Said Sameera, trying to take Veera's mind off the bell.

Veera looked both thoughtful and doubtful for a second or two, but then her face broke out in a huge mischievous grin. She looked back at Rohaan, still smiling cruelly. Rohaan literally cowered with fear and looked terrified for a few seconds before Veera pounced on him. While Veera tickled Rohaan and he screamed and vice versa, Sid ebbed closer to Sameera. 'Do you also reckon like me that Veera seems to be a bit tensed, especially when we were talking about the bell and stuff?' He asked her quietly so that Veera would not hear.

'Yeah. I think that dream is still on her mind. She is always very carefree and is never this cautious.' Replied Sameera, barely moving her lips. 'I don't know. Maybe...' However, before Sid could complete his thought, Rohaan turned towards them. 'Sameera! Tell your sister to stop tickling me!' He moaned breathlessly. Sameera got up and shook Veera's shoulders roughly and said 'Whoa, whoa! Don't tickle him to death now, Veera!'

Veera let go of Rohaan with reluctance, as the other three could tell. 'Guys! Can we please go to Rohaan and Sid's suite? It has been quite a while since I had the heavenly awesome mango smoothie that the butler...what was his name again? Oh yeah, Matt, serves!' Pleaded Veera, making a puppy face. 'You just had it this morning!' Said Sameera incredulously.

'But let's go anyway. I want to beat Rohaan here, at chess.' She added, smiling sweetly in Rohaan's direction. 'Oh God! Why do the Maheshwari sisters hate me so much? First, the younger one, Ms. Veera, tickles me nonstop, almost to death, and then the elder one, Ms. Sameera, with her nonstop nonsense during the game, will bore me almost to death. Oh

God, why me?' Moaned Rohaan, burying his face in one of the pillows from the couch. Sid and Sameera laughed heartily, Veera booed Rohaan, Rohaan grumbled some more and together, the four friends made their way to Rohaan and Sid's deluxe suite, which was awaiting them.

'What happened? Why was the AES bell used?' Gasped Captain Peterson, bustling into the meeting room where all the staff, correction. all the staff excluding waiters, gym trainers, spa people etcetera, those who knew what the bell meant were present. He got some puzzled looks for the use of abbreviation 'AES'.

'What I meant is,' He started hurriedly, 'That why was the Alarmingly Emergent Situation bell used?'

'Sir,' started Mr. Krishnamurthy, with having an air of uttering something very unpleasant. The Captain had an intuition that he was not at all going to like what the man in front of him was going to say. 'The propeller problem was bigger than we imagined. The propeller has stopped functioning properly. The reverse and direction change systems are also not working properly.'

The Captain nodded, though he did have a flicker of relief inside him. This is not that bad, he thought. It is all right. And even the most profound coincidences of coincidences cannot be of such that we would require to reverse or change directions when the systems are not working. The discussion had started again in the room and the captain forced himself to wrench out from his thoughts and listen to what Mr. Krishnamurthy was saying. 'Another mechanical engineer perhaps, Edward or Logan…' But he was rudely interrupted by a man in a pinstriped suit and check tie, whom the Captain recognized as a member Alastor of the supervising team appointed to assist Mr. Mathieu in the engines. 'I still cannot see the reason Cedric can't assist in fixing the propeller.' He said with an air of superiority around him.

'Well, he reasons that it is so because he…' a frustrated Mr. Krishnamurthy had broken off with a warning glare directed at him: courtesy of the Captain. He had been about to let the cat out of the bag and spill beans over why Cedric Rodriguez cannot come and start fixing the propeller. 'Yeah? Because he…what?' prompted Alastor. Mr. Krishnamurthy swallowed deeply and stole half a glance at the Captain before continuing. 'That is because he is busy!' 'And I take it that you know what he is 'busy' with?' Said Alastor, crossing his arms over his chest, with his tone making it clear that he didn't believe one word of what Mr. Krishnamurthy said. God, the Captain wanted to punch this man. But before he could complete his sudden wish, Alastor started talking again.

'And don't say that it is your and Cedric's personal business, because the sort of relationship between the both of you is a completely formal and professional one. So don't try to butt in when I am not interested in hearing all of your stupid explanations.'

'ALASTOR! You are crossing all your limits!' Shouted the Captain, losing all of his patience and humbleness now. Mr. Krishnamurthy had gone very-very white. One of his hands was clutching the table behind him and the other was grasping his blue shirt's fabric, right above his heart. 'Never,' he gasped, and his voice shook uncontrollably. 'Never, in twenty-four years of my career, have I been insulted to that limit.' He took a deep, calming breath. 'But that, by any means, doesn't mean that I shall tolerate your disobedience and insubordination towards your senior officials or any other member of the crew on this ship. Day after tomorrow, when the ship will be made to dock for fuelling purposes, you along with all your luggage and belongings will disembark first, never to come back abroad. In other, more clear and specific words—you are fired, Mr. Alastor.' The room went deadly silent. No one dared say anything because everyone knew that Mr. Krishnamurthy's anger was at its exploding point. Alastor visibly paled and burst into tears. He went past Mr. Krishnamurthy and ran from the room, now positively howling. The Captain distinctly heard a man saying to another 'Is Mr. Krishnamurthy serious?'

Just on the cue, somehow as if to fill Mr. Alastor's absence, Jog, who had the night's guard duty along with another man, opened the door and burst through it. He evidently didn't know that he would run into these many people because he stopped dead in his tracks, surprised. The Captain didn't think it was normal for him to be surprised, as he knew what the bell that had been rung earlier this evening meant, but obviously couldn't attend the meeting due to his duty. 'What did I miss?' Jog said slowly, as though he was still trying to contemplate the fact that all of them had been able to make it to the emergency meeting. 'It is considered polite to knock on a door before entering, maybe you missed that.' Snapped Mr. Krishnamurthy. Jog looked taken aback, and the Captain sighed internally before saying in a small yet tiring voice, 'What happened, Jog? Is it something urgent? Because if it is not, then can we please talk later in my office? We are in the middle of something. If you will please excuse us.'

Jog looked troubled, but he shook his head. 'No sir!' He cried. 'There is urgency in the situation that has arisen. A huge iceberg has been spotted. If we can reverse or change the direction of the ship immediately, only then crashing with the iceberg can be avoided.'

The Captain felt like Jog had slapped him. He heard many gasps, many shouts and whispers of, 'Oh My God!'

His insides lurched over, and then suddenly, the next moment, he felt like he didn't have any insides at all. Jog was looking thoroughly bemused. 'First, the Alarmingly Emergent Situation bell was rung and now all of you look worried. Is everything all right?' He said uncertainly. 'Alright! Nothing is all right!' Shrieked a woman. Then very gently, Mr. Krishnamurthy revealed the fact about why everyone had been so worried. 'The thing is,' He started, trying to sound calm and commanding and not frantic and worried, but failing miserably. 'The technologies and systems which enable the ship to change directions and reverse its current direction, is not functioning properly. They can start functioning again by tomorrow afternoon, at the earliest.'

Jog gave a cry of shock. 'What! I don't believe it, horrible Cedric! Where is Rodriguez? I am sure he'd be able to wait a second. He also knows what the bell means, right? Why isn't he here?' Demanded Jog. 'Well, he is busy!' Stammered Mr. Krishnamurthy nervously. The Captain wanted to murder himself and Mr. Krishnamurthy. He was going to get the whole thing caught if he did nct act a bit more convincing. I should have known, thought the Captain bitterly, the man is terrible with lies. But he chided himself immediately. Here they were on the verge of terrible trouble and death and here he was, more worried about his image and whether or not Mr. Krishnamurthy will be able to keep up their cover story.

Jog looked outraged. 'Busy? What the hell.'

'Language, Mr. McDonald,' snapped someone (the Captain was too preoccupied to find out who the voice belonged to).

'What is more important than this? Our lives; his life is at risk and he says he is busy! Does he have a death wish? Because, if he does, I can happily comply with it!'

'Mr. Jogger Kent McDonald! Cedric Rodriguez could not attend the emergency meeting because he is as lifeless as a chair in the room right now! Yes, I am sick and tired of denying this again, and again, and again! But the truth,' Mr. Krishnamurthy said glaring around all of them, silently daring them to contradict him. 'But the truth is that he is as dead and lifeless as one can be.' There were cries of shock; gasps were echoed across the room. Jog looked thoroughly shaken as he said in a very small voice 'I am sorry for behaving so childishly, sir.'

Luc*as was the first person to recover from his shock (he didn't get any shock in the first place; he already knew about Cedric from the beginning, the Captain had to remind himself). 'I zink,' He began in a very tentative sort of voice. 'Zat instead of lamenting on somzzing which is already done, and cannot be undone or reversed, 'e should focus on ze situation zat 'as arisen.'*

The Captain snapped on hearing Lucas's words. He was the person in command here, he thought, he was supposed to be keeping calm and not let his crew and passengers become panic-stricken and shell-shocked. He had to find solutions because he always had them, for each and every problem. He cleared his throat loudly and began speaking in what he thought was a commanding and instructive voice. 'Alright. So here the fact is, the thing that was supposed to happen has already happened. And, we cannot change a fact. So I want all of you to put your best tonight, because this night, the task isn't going to be easy at all.' He took a deep breath and tried not to look at the awed and scared faces of those who were being addressed by him. 'Milan and Jake, I want both of you to leave immediately for my office. There you shall find a red file in the top drawer of my reading table, labeled as 'C.P.I'. Bring it to Mr. Krishnamurthy's office and leave it on his desk. Then go to the second deck, and inform Arthur, who must be near the passage between the second deck and northeast Side of cabins, to meet me in the main conference hall in about one hour. Stay there only with Arthur for the time being. Off you go, you are dismissed.' Jake and Milan both nodded and hurried out of the door.

'Antonin and Anthony, I want both of you to go to the engines immediately and bring all the blueprints of internal ship designs especially of the propeller's position and engines to Mr. Mathieu here. Behave

quite normally, as if nothing has happened and all is in order. We don't want the workers to be panicking, do we? Then go to the main deck where you shall find Helena in the passageway leading to the infirmary, and tell her that she is required in the main conference hall in the next hour. Don't stay with Helena, come back here right away.' Both of them also hurried out of the door. Next he turned to Mr. Mathieu.

'Mathieu, you will stay here. Keep sending me hourly reports on what is happening. Send your best team of mechanical engineers down to the engines to inspect the propeller. I am sure one of them must know a solution to the problem we are currently facing. Other than that, tell one of the cleaning guys to tidy the main conference hall; we'd be having a meeting there in another one hour. You are also to be there. And prepare some distress signal rockets. In case they are needed tonight...just keep them ready for firing OK. All clear?'

Mr. Mathieu nodded and confirmed the gesture with an 'All clear,' 'Ah, Krishnamurthy, would you mind accompanying me to your office, seeing that we have some matters to discuss and situations to solve.' Said the Captain looking at Mr. Krishnamurthy, who still looked pretty furious. His mouth was set in a thin line, his fists were clenched and his teeth were pressed together so tightly that the Captain was quite certain that they must be hurting. He nodded and left the room with the Captain. 'Jesus, just get us out of this mess. Because if we are not able to get out, then it would be likely that many people are going to die.' Whispered Mr. Mathieu, looking at the photo of his wife and two children in his wallet.

'Why did you do that?' Half-shouted the Captain as soon as he and Mr. Krishnamurthy were out of earshot of the people assembled in the meeting room right now. 'Why did I do what?' Asked Mr. Krishnamurthy in a deadly calm sort of voice. 'You know perfectly well what you did! You disclosed the secret about why Cedric Rodriguez wasn't able to attend the emergency meetings or assist in fixing the propeller and reverse systems! We agreed on disposing of the body.'

'Yeah? And what good will that do to anybody? The propeller's not functioning, and it is obvious that this ship shall sink.'

'Shekhar Krishnamurthy! That is not going to happen. Cedric wasn't such a great mechanical engineer that the ship's engines cannot go a day through without him!'

'I don't care if he was a great mechanical engineer or not. I just know that Cedric Rodriguez was a man with a feeling of empathy, kindness and goodness to each and every being he ever encountered. He was a great friend, brother, mentor and most importantly, a great human with a sense of humanity like no other. You may not think so, but I certainly think that he deserved a better sendoff than people tagging the plate of 'Irresponsible' in front of his name. And as for the ship, both you and I know that it is going to sink. The only difference is, you refuse to accept it and I already have. I suggest you inform each and every soul aboard about the disaster and let everyone enjoy the little amount of time left with their loved ones who they, if not they are extremely lucky, might lose forever.'

8

'Gentlemen.'

'And Ladies!'

'Yes. Ladies and Gentlemen, you must have heard about the current dilemma that we are facing surely, so I will not bother explaining it. Our team of mechanical engineers have already checked the propeller and concluded that the amount of damage it has suffered due to apparently unknown reasons, it, nevertheless, cannot be fixed on such short notice, and minimum until tomorrow.' Said The Captain curtly. He had been addressing all the faculty members who would be overseeing evacuations: discharge of lifeboats, firing of rockets to grab any nearby ship's attention that they were in trouble, sending of help messages to all ships in a certain radius et cetera.

'Now, about the plan of evacuation. I have already ordered the discharge of lifeboats and fire of rockets. The only problem remaining is handling the passengers. They would, no doubt, panic. And panicking in such an extreme situation can prove fatal. So I would suggest all of you, and the rest of the crew to work and give their best for keeping the situation under control. The passengers will

be loaded on to lifeboats from the lower deck and second deck only. Use of the main deck for any purposes whatsoever is strictly prohibited. I shall station several crew members on the main deck, who will disembark only after the crowd of passengers has lessened.

We shall be crashing into the iceberg in about half an hour. Due to it not being in the path of the ship's direction, the left side of our starboard will crash into the iceberg. We have conducted evacuation drills for the passengers to know which emergency passageway they have to use, based upon in which section of cabins, the cabin they are occupying is located. I shall again read out the duty list. Milan and Anthony: both of you shall be stationed at exit B, from where only the southeast Side of cabins of the second deck shall pass. You will receive your box of life jackets, which you shall ensure that each passenger is properly wearing before letting them pass. Clear? OK, good. Next, George and Katie: both of you will be at exit D, from which only deluxe suite occupants shall pass. I shall be giving both of you a list of all such occupants; you will ask them the sign as soon as they pass. And your pack of life jackets shall also be given to you. Now this information is for all the other crew members who shall be hosting non-deluxe occupants, do not let any deluxe suite occupant go through your respective passages. Ask each of the passing passengers if they are deluxe occupants or not. Now, for the rest of the list ...'

'I really don't know how the passengers will react to this. It might come as a shocker.' Frowned Jog, in such a way that only Lucas, who was standing beside him, could hear. 'Yeah. I dunno what ze captain was thinking, when 'e told us zat we were supposed to keep zem calm and all.' Whispered Lucas back, after a moment or two. Jog nodded but didn't reply back. He forced himself to actually listen to what the Captain was saying. '....so, that was our entire evacuation plan. Any questions?' He finished with his speech and clasped his hands, looking around to see if there were any raised hands. 'Ah, yes Luna?'

'Sir, you see, I actually have two questions.'

'Ask away, my dear.'

'Both of my queries are based upon life jackets. My first one is, just assume that the life jackets delivered to us on our respective duty exits are not enough, and we are forced to ask for more, are there extra life jackets available, as per the number of people, including the crew onboard?' Luna asked the question with a tentative voice and carefully chose her words, as she didn't know which ones might end

up offending the Captain. He, however, didn't seem to be upset or offended. On the contrary, he nodded gravely like he had expected the question.

'You see, on the subject, I do have something to share with you guys.' He gestured towards all of them and said the statement with an air of uttering something unpleasant, bitter and dislikable. 'The crew is one great family, who resides abroad the ship. And there is no hiding from the family. But, the next few lines that I speak will remain within this room only and in strictest confidence. The passengers are not to be known about this, by any means, direct or indirect. There aren't enough life jackets, or lifeboats for that matter, for the number of people on board. This means that for some people onboard, it shall be the last few hours of their life.' A stunned silence greeted his words.

This situation feels exactly like that of 'Titanic' accident thaught Milan to himself. Then suddenly, Mr. Mathieu stood up and pointed a shaking finger at the Captain. He looked quite outraged, unlike his usual calm and disciplined self. 'I did keep a requirement during the board meeting before this ship set sail that there should be life jackets and lifeboats available in such a number that there is one for each soul onboard! You kept telling me that it was done and that I have nothing to worry about. And now you are saying that there are not enough lifeboats and life jackets! How could you?' He asked hysterically. The Captain grabbed his shoulders, but Mr. Mathieu wrenched himself out of his grasp. *'My dear man, do you honestly think that I would have a greater priority than making sure of the passengers' protection?'* He said weakly.

'Personally speaking, I think I do.' Muttered George, to himself. Mr. Mathieu looked away, unable to say anything. The Captain grabbed this opportunity to defend and justify himself. But before he could put two cents in, he was interrupted by Lucas. *'Sirs, I zink zat ze time is ebbing away. If we continue to argue on ze matters, which are simply out of control, we shall be putting ourselves and ze passengers in an even graver situation.'* He said logically. Mr. Mathieu took a deep and calming breath and said in a tight, curt voice *'I think what the boy is saying is sensible. Right, all of you are dismissed. Ryan, go and ring the emergency bell which is only used when we need the passengers to assemble in any of both the decks. Except for the crew members who have gotten passage duties, everyone else shall manage the crowd, who will gather on the Lower and Second decks.'*

Everyone nodded and left to do their respective jobs. Jog caught up with his group of friends, consisting of Lucas, Helena, Luna and Jake. 'Hi everyone,' He said, leaning against the passageway wall. Helena and Luna gave him weak smiles, Lucas clapped his back and Jake said 'Hey, man!' 'I don't believe it guys,' Said Luna softly. 'You don't believe what?' Asked Jake curiously. But Jog knew what Luna was talking about. 'This ship it has been our home for several weeks. And now, it is going to sink, probably taking lives of hundreds with her.' She said, proving Jog right.

'We also don't know whether we will be one of those hundreds or not.' Said Helena, tears starting to form in her deep blue eyes. 'Awww, come on, group hug,' Said Lucas. All of them wrapped their arms; no one could tell your arms were wrapped around whom or whose arms were wrapped around you. At that moment, Jog truly understood how precious life was to them. How he had taken everything, from his mum and Dad, to his own small apartment in Southampton to this friendship of Helena, Jake, Lucas and Luna for granted. As they say, you never truly understand the value of something until it is gone. Thinking that, a few tears gathered in his eyes too, but instead of pretending that they weren't there or wiping them, he let them fall.

'Blimey, I can walk in everyday and still not get used to a suite as big as this,' Said Veera, looking around Rohaan and Sid's suite in awe. Sameera nodded vigorously as she plopped herself down on the couch. 'Guys, you want to watch a movie? I have a laptop.' Said Sid, rummaging through his backpack. 'Consider me in.' Said Rohaan and Veera-Sameera agreed too. 'Hey! Let us watch Finding Nemo,' Said Rohaan excitedly. Veera looked as if she was trying very hard on not trying to roll her eyes and Sameera burst or laughing.

'Seventeen-year-old and still suggesting Finding Nemo?' She wheezed, clutching her Sides. 'What? Any person of any age can watch it. Movies are not for a particular age group.' Said Rohaan defensively. 'Oh shut up, you two! And Sid, don't try to stifle your laughter, you will end up choking. Now go on, put on Finding Nemo.' Instructed Veera. Sameera whirled around to get a better look at Veera, her laughter forgotten. 'We are going to watch Finding Nemo? Like, seriously?' She said incredulously. Veera shrugged lightly before saying 'I have never watched it before. Though I know it is an animated movie for children,'

'Oh My God! You have never watched Finding Nemo. What are you living for, Veera Maheshwari?'

Said Rohaan, while gaping at her. Veera scowled deeply and threw a cushion from the couch at Rohaan, who ducked to avoid it. 'Missed,' He said gleefully, failing to notice Veera's second throw, and getting hit in the face from a pink cushion. 'Hit,' said Veera triumphantly, straightening her shirt's collars proudly.

Sameera interrupted before it could turn into a furious cushion fight, and motioned Sid to start the movie, who was standing with his backpack in one hand, watching the entire Veera-Rohaan show with a mildly amused expression. Half an hour later, Sameera and Sid were fast asleep, both having watched the movie numerous times when they were children. Veera and Rohaan, however, were wide awake and hanging on every word the characters spoke. Suddenly, an alarm went off somewhere, but its shrillness made sure that it was well heard in every cabin or suite.

But unlike the first time, Veera this time knew what the Alarm Bell signified. Some days previously, an evacuation drill had been conducted to make the passengers come to know that whenever this bell rang, everyone had to leave whatever work they had been doing and head to the exit, which was classified on the basis of which cabin they occupied. 'Oi!

Wake up!' She almost shouted, shaking Sameera and swatting Sid's arm. Sameera woke up with a start and looked around, thoroughly confused. 'Wassamatter?' Said Sid, groggily, fighting to keep his eyes open.

'The Alarm Bell is the matter, sleepyheads!' Said Veera, abandoning her hold on Sameera's shoulder, seeing that she was awake now. 'What about it?' Asked Sameera sleepily. Veera groaned, but instead of replying, turned her attention towards Rohaan, who was gaping at the laptop, completely open-mouthed. 'Rohaan Parimal! I am telling you that if you didn't switch off that damn laptop, then I will throw you in the ocean.' Said Veera, completely exhausted. 'The Alarm Bell just went off a few minutes ago, and it means that all of us have to head off for the Exit.

As Rohaan was locking the door and Sameera was standing with him, ensuring that he did it properly, Sid noticed Veera looking worried. 'You are looking tensed up. All okay?' He asked softly, approaching her. 'I don't know. First that dream and now this....I have a very bad feeling about this, Sid.' Said Veera tensely. Sid nodded, showing that he understood, and placed his hand on her shoulder, squeezing it in a reassuring sort of way. 'It's okay.

Nothing bad will happen to you. I think this a sort of surprise drill, to test whether you paid any attention to the instructions the crew gave us in the last drill or not. You know, umm, like the surprise tests our teachers spring on us every other day to torture us? Like that only.' He said in a soothing voice, trying to make her laugh. And he was successful in it too. Veera gave a small laugh and some, if not all, lines of tension had slipped of her face.

They separated to go through their respective passages and when they united on the second deck, everything was....chaos. There were cries of fear, the sounds of lifeboats being lowered into water, the blasts of rockets being fired. In one spiraling moment it seemed to hit the four of them: this was no practice, this was the real thing. There ship was sinking, and there was no denying it. It was just as if Veera's dream had come as a warning, to enjoy the last few hours on the ship. Veera heard Sameera stifle a cry, Rohaan cursing and swearing angrily and Sid gasping. But she couldn't express her fear in actions or through gestures because her enmities seemed to have gone numb. A grieving sensation seemed to be spreading through her brain and body, paralyzing her with shock. Sameera however seemed to have found her voice and opened her mouth to say something. But what, Veera never found out.

At that moment, one of the pillars supporting the railing around the deck gave a violent jerk and came crashing down. People screamed and ran for their dear lives. Veera, Sameera, Sid and Rohaan, who had been standing right under the pillar, tried to escape. Rohaan, Sid and Veera managed to do so unhurt, but Sameera was not so lucky. She just managed to escape but the pillar hit the wooden deck so hard that she was thrown off balance. She stumbled right into the railing, which surprisingly broke and Sameera stumbled, and fell into the vast blue ocean. 'No! Sameera Di! Di! No, no, no!' Screamed Veera, trying to run towards the missing iron bars in the railing. Both Sid and Rohaan grabbed her and tried to restrain her from jumping down to the ocean. There were tears sliding down there cheeks too. Oh god, thought Rohaan despairingly. How will her parents react to his? Sameera was a great friend and sister. Was-past tense. Her knees gave away after minutes of screaming and tears. She sank into the floor in a heap of anguished and heartbroken sobs. She was still saying 'Sameera Di...' But she also, somewhere deep down, knew that Sameera had gone somewhere from where, even Veera couldn't call her back.

9

There were no words perhaps to describe how Veera was feeling at the moment. Broken. Hollow. Empty. 'Come on, Veera. Let us go and get a lifeboat.' Said Sid half-heartedly. 'Sameera Di...Sameera...' Sobbed Veera, putting her face in her hands. Rohaan silently mouthed Sid to pull Veera up and take her to the other side of the deck where the lifeboats were being lowered. Sid and Rohaan grabbed an arm each of Veera and put them around their shoulders. They then encircled her waist with their remaining free hand and started to move towards the opposite side of the deck. Veera made no attempt to do otherwise and sobbed quietly into Rohaan's shoulder, heavily leaning on both the boys.

'Women and Children first, please! No sir, only women and children first! Please, women and children this way!' Shouted a man clad in a navy uniform. Then he spotted Sid, Rohaan and Veera standing there. 'All under eighteen?' He asked and when Rohaan nodded, he said 'This way please. Robert, lower that lifeboat. This way please, sirs and madam.' He gestured towards a cue, where

half a dozen women and about a dozen kids were standing.

'Veera, we need to join the cue. Will it be OK if...?' Whispered Rohaan softly in Veera's ear. For a moment or two, it appeared as if she didn't hear him, but after that she quietly freed herself from Rohaan and Sid's grasps and moved on to stand between them in the cue. Her cheeks were tear-streaked and her eyes were rimmed red. Her sobs had been reduced to hiccups, but she still looked on the verge of breaking down. Sid looked at Veera sympathetically, his eyes full of pity for her. Both Sid and Rohaan knew how close had Veera and Sameera been and how much Sameera mattered to Veera. On the cue, Veera turned towards Rohaan.

'Turns out that the dream I had earlier was true indeed, huh?' She said in a bitter sort of voice, unlike her usual carefree and sweet one. Rohaan shook his head, not sure about how to respond to that statement. 'Hey, Veera, your life jacket's strings are not fastened properly. Want me to do them for you?' Said Sid kindly. Veera nodded and let Sid do the fastenings, though Rohaan was sure that Sid only suggested it to take Veera's mind off things because when Veera turned her back to Sid, her jacket's straps had been done as properly as

before. Suddenly, Veera's head shot up, as if she had just got an idea. 'Sameera Di is wearing a life jacket, right?' She asked Rohaan, tugging his arm impatiently.

'Is? You mean...' Sid broke off with a warning glare from Rohaan. It would have been pretty insensitive of him to correct Veera on her tense usage when she was in such a weakened condition. But Veera, who had eyes only for Rohaan, appeared to have not heard Sid's comment. 'Umm, yeah. Why?' Said Rohaan, gaping at her. 'Well, if she is wearing a life jacket then she would not have drowned. She would have eventually floated only. Some lifeboats had already been lowered at that time. She must have screamed for help, and any lifeboat in the vicinity would have come and rescued her.' Said Veera.

Rohaan considered this possibility. All the lifeboats were being lowered at the other side of the deck and with the water currents, there as little possibility that her screams of help would be heard all the way there. The water must be so cold that it would be nearly impossible to stay in the freezing water for longer than about fifteen minutes. She would either get hypothermia or go in a coma because of the body's temperatures coming down.

But he didn't want to crash all of Veera's hopes so he gave a small nod and said, 'Yeah! That is possible!'

Veera seemed satisfied with the answer. She clung on to the minor possibility, just like a ray of hope. They stood in silence for about five minutes more, but it seemed to be an eternity. Veera was lost in her grief for Sameera, Sid didn't trust himself to say anything to Veera as she feared to say something which would upset her even more.

*Rohaan wanted to tell Veera that everything would be OK eventually, but he could not do so for two reasons: (a) that of course using the word 'OK' in the light of recent events would be pretty insensitive and ridiculous and (b) no such words of consolation occurred to him. After what felt like forever, the man with a nametag reading **James** gestured to Veerasaid 'Yes Ma'am, you are next person to board the lifeboat. While climbing make sure to hold the ropes with a firm grip. After sitting, don't forget to tie the belt securely. If you are unable to do so, our helping crew will be happy to assist. Robert, it is Ma'am next.'*

Veera blinked as if coming out of a trance and said 'Sorry, if you could please repeat,' Sid cut Veera off and offered to go first and show Veera how to do it. After carefully climbing up, he offered his hand to Veera. She took it and after she had sat down safely only then did Rohaan climb up. A few more people joined them and then very slowly, the nails were released and the ropes were cut and gradually, the lifeboat settled itself on the high tides. 'I hope that Mumma and Dad make it safely to the ship rescuing us.' Said Veera in such a quiet voice that Rohaan and Sid almost didn't hear her.

'They would have. I am sure of it.' Said Sid comfortingly. Veera gave a small nod and tears started flowing down her cheeks again. 'God, Veera,' Said Rohaan and he put an arm around the now openly crying girl; she leaned on to him as Sid rubbed soothing circles on her back and whispered reassurances to her. Tears were again beginning to pool in her black eyes, as she took a gasp of the air; her first sob racked through her body. 'What will happen-hic-if mum-hic-and Dad are not-hic-there on the ship-hic-rescuing us? It would-hic-mean that they are-hic-d-dead?' She said between sobs, her voice muffled by Rohaan's sleeve.

'It will be fine. Remember what you said? Sameera will make it. And as for aunty and uncle, they are going to make it. I know it.' Whispered Rohaan, ruffling her hair. Veera lifted her head up and wiped her nose noisily on the sleeve of her white flowery

frock. 'I am getting your jacket wet.' She moaned, pointing her index finger towards Rohaan's black hoodie, whose one side was soaked with Veera's tears. 'Seriously?' Said Rohaan incredulously. But an idea hit him and decided to follow it.

'It's OK if it is torn, but it better not be nose drool, OK?' He said in a light threatening tone, trying to make her laugh. She half laughed and half sobbed, but the next moment, she turned somber once more and looked away. 'Look, we are approaching SS Marina.' Said Sid pointing in Rohaan's direction.

Rohaan looked over his shoulder to see a massive ship about a hundred yards away. Thousands of light, probably of the cabins, were glittering. The light-emitting was so strong that the blue water surrounding the ship was also visible as a vast blue blanket. As the lifeboat surged towards it, Rohaan glanced towards Sid. His eyes looked sad and full of sympathy and pity for, obviously, Veera. He kept sneaking glances at her (just like Rohaan was doing for, both Veera and his brother) to see if her mood was OK or not and if she had stopped crying or not. How did the childish and 'stupid in matters of feelings' Sid he knew to turn out to be so mature and understanding in just a period of a few hours, wondered Rohaan. He wasn't saying that he was a great saint when it came to feelings and all, but at least he was better than Sid, at times. But even better than both of them in this subject was Sameera.

Oh God, Sameera. 'Sameera is dead,' He mumbled slowly, such that Veera wouldn't hear. The words made no sense, and if someone would have said them to Rohaan a few hours ago, he would have thought that either he had drunk too much of liquor or that he was completely psycho and was a runaway person of the mental asylum. Sameera knew exactly how to cheer up a person, how to make someone smile so widely that all of their teeth would be visible. She was also damn annoying at times and irritate anyone so much that they would go completely nuts. She was a good friend, a good sister, a good daughter and most important of all, a good human being. She was filled with humanity and compassion and goodness for everyone.

If I am missing her so much, then I can't even imagine what Veera will be going through and what her parents will go through when they find out that their eldest daughter is no more, thought Rohaan sadly. They had a relation of blood with Sameera. 'What am I going to say to Mumma and Dad when they ask me where is Sameera Di?' Choked Veera. She seemed to be talking to herself more than Sid or Rohaan. 'Hey, you don't...wouldn't need to say anything. They will understand without you saying anything. I am sure it.' Whispered Rohaan. 'Mumma will break down.' Said Veera hoarsely.

'It is understandable. But you will have to ensure one thing. You will not break down in front of Aunty and Uncle, OK? You have to remain strong for them. For a man and woman who lost their beloved daughter. She was the apple of their eye; the jewel of their family. You have to remain strong and not shed a single tear, even if you are breaking down inside. For your mum. For your Dad. And most importantly, for Sameera. It would have killed her to see her little sister falling apart and her parents in so much agony.' Said Rohaan, swallowing the lump in his throat. His chest constricted, tears started to form in his eyes. He let them fall; they showed that he was in pain for Veera and that he sincerely understood what she was going through. He looked at Sid and saw tears sliding down his cheeks too. He looked away, unable to look at either of them. He saw a young boy crying and holding his mother. 'Mom, will Daddy be able to make it?' He asked quietly. His mom gave him a sad, watery smile and placed a kiss on his forehead. 'It will all be OK, son. Christ is with us,' she said, hugging him and wiping

her tears over his shoulder, such that he wouldn't see. It was fate only, thought Rohaan bitterly. Fate had torn apart these families, ruined these lives….

'Come, ahoy!' Yelled a gruff voice. Rohaan looked in the direction of the voice to see a middle-aged man with a fairly round belly yelling through a handheld megaphone. 'Lifeboat number twelve on arrival. Oi! Jeff! Boy, get those bleeding towels and refreshments. And send word to the captain that almost half of the bleeding people have arrived.'

He yelled again, lowering the megaphone, but now that they were quite close to the platform, Rohaan could hear him quite clearly. The crew member rowing the lifeboat grabbed the rope and threw it to a young boy who was standing near the edge of the platform. He caught it and tied it across a sort of rod. As soon as he did it, the man rowing the boat docked it safely and stood up. 'Now, sirs and madams, we are now going to be sheltered at the SS Marina, whose kind and gracious, Captain Patrick Summers Jr. has allowed us to use the amenities his ship offers to their passengers. We shall be docking at the port of Cape Town in the predicted time.

I suggest all of you freshen yourselves, while the crew will take you to the accommodations made for you. I think a good sleep shall help you recover, if not fully then partially, from the trauma you have undergone. The entire list of the survivors will be out on the morning of the day after tomorrow. I will also suggest, actually request, all of you not to haphazardly search for your relatives. This will not contribute to making the situation under control. Rather, it shall help in increasing fear, chaos and confusion.

The crew, of both SS Marina and The Royal Eureka, are trying their hardest to find solutions, but naturally, time will be taken. We are extremely sorry for any inconvenience caused and request you to cooperate with us. Thank you so much.' Said a man, who had just descended to the platform. He waved a careless hand behind him, and at once, a dozen waiters or so moved forward, holding plates full of bread and cheese, mugs of hot cocoa and coffee and warm blankets. Slowly, all the occupants of the lifeboat climbed out. Immediately, the waiters offered them the eateries and warm liquids, along with soft and comfortable blankets. Rohaan took three blankets; gave one to Sid who wrapped it around himself, wrapped one around Veera, seeing that she was still staring into space to take one and do it herself and wrapped the last one around himself. Sid then took two cups full of hot cocoa, handed one to Veera and the other to his brother and took one for himself. When the waiters offered them bread and cheese, Rohaan turned to Veera.

'Do you want something to eat, Veera?' He asked quietly. When she denied needing any, Rohaan turned towards their servicemen and said 'Send three plates of bread and cheese to whichever room you assign to Rohaan Awasthi.' The waiter nodded and scribbled the instruction on a notepad before bowing and stepping away. The three of them then started climbing the steps leading them to the main entrance of the ship. 'I was thinking, that if the lifeboat has already safely docked us in this ship, umm, yes, the SS Marina, then why can't it go back to our ship—The Royal Eureka and come back with another batch of evacuees?' Wondered Sid.

'It doesn't work like that, Sid. The SS Marina can't take the load of all the passengers or ship. It has its own to take care of. So, our ship must have contacted various other vessels within a certain range of miles, to seek help. All the vessels that must have confirmed their helping hand will be sent certain batches of evacuees.' Explained Rohaan. Though Sid nodded, he still looked very confused. Veera seemed to have not heard a single word of the conversation both the brothers were

sharing regarding the methods of evacuation and the approach of evacuees. 'There is absolutely no need to give me that nod or look as if you have understood each and every word I said. I know you are confused. Come on now, hit me with the questions.' Said Rohaan and he could swear that he saw Veera half-smile and whether it was from his remark or recollecting some memory of herself and Sameera, he didn't know.

'Thanks, Bro. You always see the right through me. So you remember James Cameron's blockbuster movie, The Titanic?' Sid said. Raising his eyebrows suggestively. 'Yeah, I have. I remember it very well. We had watched it on Netflix around six months ago.' Said Rohaan and even though he had not heard it, he could guess what Sid's question would be.

'We did? OK, so the point is that the evacuation process shown there was completely different. Why is that?' Asked Sid, proving Rohaan correct. 'Well, for one thing, the Titanic sank in 1912, and at that time the technology was OK, not that great. For another, the class differences were there at that time and people from influential families with well-connected networks managed to corrupt several officials and secure a seat on a lifeboat. It is common knowledge

that the number of lifeboats available at that time was quite less as compared to the two thousand two hundred twenty-three souls on board.

All the capacity of lifeboats was designed to hold the weight of fifty-seventy men, but in a majority of the cases, not even half of them were completely filled.' Explained Rohaan. Sid nodded and he asked the last question that he had in his mind. 'Bro, after we have docked in Cape Town, what are we going to do?' He asked worriedly. Rohaan looked troubled as he said 'We might want to contact mum and Dad. We will tell them to book us two flights from Cape Town to Delhi. Originally we would have docked in Mumbai and mum and Dad would have come and picked us up and taken us back to Delhi. But now.... circumstances are no longer the same. They have changed severely.'

'What about Veera though?' Asked Sid. At times, that boy has an endless curiosity for things. 'Well, aunty and uncle will decide that.' Said Rohaan. 'And what if they don't.....survive?' Asked Sid quietly. Rohaan's brain took a moment to understand what Sid had asked, and when it did, the first thing that Rohaan did was to whirl around to look at Veera, to make sure that by any means she had not heard Sid's question. It would have upset her greatly that

her parent's not surviving was also a possibility. Veera seemed to be, however, lost in her own world and she didn't appear to have heard Sid's question. 'Are you crazy or something? What if Veera would have heard? She would have been so upset.' Hissed Rohaan. 'We will talk about this later, OK?' When Sid didn't respond, Rohaan repeated 'I asked, is that OK?' Sid nodded guiltily. He sneaked a glance at Veera and his guilt and sympathy, both seemed to increase. 'I know it will hurt Veera if she hears it. And I am thoroughly sorry for that. But, still, you can't deny that it can't happen or that it is not a possibility. I would be for the best only if Veera is braced for it in advance. If she isn't and it happens, either she will have a mental breakdown or she will fall apart. I can guarantee you that.'

He whispered slowly, making sure that there was no chance that Veera heard them. 'I agree. But we will give it her a day or two. She is already dealing with the loss of Sameera. If another tragedy will strike her so quickly after the first, then it shall be even more terrifying for her.' Whispered Rohaan back. 'That is the problem, bro. We don't have much time. The list of survivors will be out soon. We have to, in the best way possible, explain that it is not guaranteed that aunty and uncle will definitely survive. It's for her best only.' Said Sid. Rohaan was about to reply when…

'What would be the best and for whom?'

10

Veera was looking up to them, her hands on her hips and eyes narrowed. Sid could swear that girl could make the most confident person around her melt with insecurity both with and without that posture of hers. She was one intimidating girl, for sure. Both the boys looked at each other, both of their glances saying *it is entirely your fault; she could have heard everything* to the other before Rohaan looked away and cleared his throat loudly.

'Uh, Veera, what Sid was saying was that maybe you should, umm go and get some sleep, you must be tired, you know…' He said lamely. Veera raised her eyebrows, probably debating whether Rohaan was lying or not. Rohaan glanced at Sid, waiting for the verdict to come. After what felt like forever, Veera nodded in such a skeptical sort of way that made Rohaan hundred and one percent positive that she hadn't believed one word of the lame excuse that he had given her. Before she could question him further however, a member of the SS Marina staff appeared.

'Sirs, Madam, please come this way. Another batch of evacuees will be coming soon.' He said professionally, indicating towards the door through which he had just appeared in front of them. Sid nodded and began walking towards the door; Rohaan and Veera followed suit. They entered what seemed like a gathering hall, lots and lots of people were moving here and there and about a dozen members of the ship's staff were standing here and there; explaining groups of scandalized and frantic looking people how grave and unfortunate the current circumstances were. Sid walked towards a desk where a small and rather mousey looking woman was standing.

The words 'INQUIRY DESK' were written on the desk. 'Um, hi, this is Siddharth. Is there any kind of accommodation ready? Actually, there is a kind of urgency. So if it is available, we are ready to access it.' He said to the woman. The woman looked up and nodded. She typed something on her monitor and looked up again. 'Yes. There is accommodation ready for you and your brother, Mr. Parimal. If you could please fill this form, I will register you and you can access your room.' She said and handed Sid a form. Sid handed the form to Rohaan to fill it in return.

'Can I get a....? Yeah, a pen will do, thank. Thank you here, bro, you can write with this. Also,

I was wondering what the status of accommodation for Ms. Veera is. Veera Maheshwari?' Said Sid. The woman nodded and again typed something on her monitor. 'Yes, sir, a room has already been accommodated for Veera Ma'am. For her and her sister Ms. Sameera Maheshwari. Is that right?' Said the woman. 'Yes, that is rig…' Sid stopped mid sentence, looking horror-struck as he turned around to Veera. Her mouth was half-open as tears slid down her face. She was taking gasps for air; twisting her hands in agony. Sid looked towards Rohaan, whose eyes were full of anger for Sid and sympathy for Veera.

'Veera, come with me, please. I need a glass of water.' Said Rohaan kindly, trying to distract Veera. Sid shot an apologetic look to Rohaan as he led Veera away, trying to gain some amount of reassurance from him. Thankfully, all the anger melted from Rohaan's eyes. He seemed to have understood that whatever happened was purely coincidental and not intentional. Sid smacked himself in the head mentally for even thinking about the last part. Rohaan would never ever think that Sid would purposely do such a mistake, Sid was sure of it. But then, why was anger obvious in his eyes? He would definitely be lying is he said that he was not once jealous of Rohaan. He had always been the more handsome, intelligent and mature one...

Everybody looked up to him for advice. He sometimes thought that Rohaan was 3C's. Cool. Confident. Charming. Whereas, he was a joker. Always expected to be joking and messing around. His mum and Dad had to give up their children, just because he had been born at the wrong time. Whenever their grandmother had emotionally exhausted them, Sid would always yell up his frustration. He would scream and bellow slangs for his grandmother for hours. He would be so angry, not only with grandmother but with his mum and Dad too.

They were the ones who had sent them to their cruel and merciless grandmother, making her their legal guardians. Whenever Sid would talk about his anger on their parents, there would always be a sad smile on Rohaan's face. Every time he would manage to calm Sid down and say 'They had their own reasons. Keep faith in God. He will make everything all right.' Some people say humor helps greatly in lessening your pain. In Sid's case, humor helps greatly in hiding your pain.

'Stupid,' He muttered to himself angrily. There was Veera, who had lost her sister and probably her mum and Dad as well and here he was thinking about his own problems. Rohaan was the best bro in the entire world. And about his mum and Dad? They sacrificed everything, including their happiness for his and Rohaan's welfare and he should remain thankful to them for that. But their problems are coming to an end aren't they? We are going to go back to Mum and Dad. This is our happily ever after. Our Happy ending, thought Sid desperately. He felt bad immediately. Here he was mourning about such silly things, while Veera, she had serious problems in life. He seriously was behaving, kinda selfish? Self-centered? Yeah, probably both. 'Excuse me? If you are done then can you move aside, others are waiting in a queue you know?' Said a plump, blond woman behind him, waving her hands impatiently.

Sid snapped out of his trance and mumbled a quick sorry. He collected the form Veera was supposed to fill and hurried out of there. Plopping himself in the lounge, he began filling up Veera's form, with all the information he had about her.

'That was pretty dense of you, man.' Said Rohaan, as he came down to sit next to Sid after some time. Veera was nowhere in sight. 'I know. It is just that...I spoke without thinking, that's all. Otherwise, I would have never ever said what I said.

You know, I just can't believe that Sameera is...' He couldn't complete the sentence. He couldn't say the word *dead*. Sameera could be described as funny, beautiful, caring, innocent and a thousand more adjectives like that, but never dead. She was always so lively and a lively person can never be dead. 'I know.' Said Rohaan quietly, putting his hand on Sid's shoulder and squeezing it softly. 'No we don't.'

'What?' Said Rohaan, taken aback.

'What I said Bro is that we don't even know the half of it! Veera has just lost her beloved sister. And consolation isn't going to help in decreasing or lessening her pain!' Snapped Sid. He expected Rohaan to retort even angrily, or snap back at him. After all, even though he was patient, no one could tolerate it if someone accused them unreasonably. Now that Sid came to think of it, even he didn't know why he was feeling so snappy. But to his immense surprise, Rohaan nodded.

'You are right. We don't know any of it. The pain that you feel....it is terrible. Outer wounds heal with time, but inner wounds....they take a lifetime to. Physical pain is much, much more bearable then mental and emotional pain.' He said. Time to lighten things up, Sid thought. We need to stand strong and positive for Veera. 'Spoken like a true philosopher, man.' He said. Rohaan half-smiled and looked away. They sat in silence for a long period of time; Rohaan staring here and there, observing his surroundings and fellow rescues and Sid trying to fill up Veera's form and failing miserably. After a long time, Sid finally completed his form filling and got up to submit it to the lady at the inquiry desk. When he returned, Rohaan looked up gloomily from his observations. 'Where is Veera?' Sid asked half-heartedly. 'She went to one of the cafes to grab a bagel.' Rohaan explained. Sid raised his eyebrows, surprised that Veera had agreed so easily. Rohaan seemed to have understood what was going on in his younger brother's mind, for he smiled slightly and said 'It took some convincing and some forcing on my part.'

The morning sun glowed a few days later, wishing the recently put to rest minds a good day. Rohaan had tossed and turned all night, unable to get any sleep. He knew that the same thing happened with Sid, he could feel him tossing and turning all night in the bed beside him. A thousand thoughts clouded his mind: some of them were so crazy that they sounded stupid inside his head as well. He had considered waking Sid up and asking what was he thinking about, but had dropped the idea a few minutes after brooding over it. He didn't want Sid to think that he was himself thinking about the fateful evening when he had just told him not to do so. But indeed it was very difficult not to do so. After all, how many people lived to say 'Hey, did you know that I survived a sinking ship? Cool, right?'

Not many. Just the sight of Sameera slipping and falling down kept replaying, just like someone had pressed a button to keep playing it. And then there was Veera herself. Her petrified, white as a chalk face didn't seem to go away from in front of his eyes. And then there was the thought of her parents as well. If they made it, it would definitely kill them to see their elder daughter gone and younger one completely shattered and distraught. Finally, after hours, his eyes had drooped and he had started to slip into the primary state of unconsciousness. Now, very suddenly his eyes snapped open as there was a rap on the door. His vision was blurry and unclear due to the fact that he had just woken up, but he still managed to slant his eyes and look at the time in his cellphone. 6:28 a.m.

Who the heck is knocking at this time, thought Rohaan groggily as he got up from the bed and made his way towards the door? He jerked it open, only to find that there was no one standing there.

He poked his head out of the door and looked left and right, only to reach the same conclusion that no one was there. He was about to lock the door when he found an envelope on the floor. Curious, he picked it. There it was, written in a neat and sleek handwriting:

Conclusion of the search report of

Mr. and Mrs. Maheshwari

It was as if somebody had dumped a bucket of freezing water on Rohaan's head on a cool winter morning. His fingers started trembling as he held the envelope, knowing that it was a very crucial paper in Veera's life. He ran back inside, his heart hammering loudly in his chest, threatening to burst out. 'SID! Wake up! Oi! Sid!' He shouted, grabbing Sid's sheets and flinging hem down the bed. Sid grunted as he turned to face him. 'Whassamatter?' He said groggily. 'This!' Shouted Rohaan as he thrust the envelope onto Sid's hand. He looked confused for a second, but then his eyes widened severely. He sat down quickly, all sleepiness forgotten. 'Oh My God! I don't...can't...believe this.' Said Sid looking scared. Rohaan nodded and said 'I know. The day we both have been praying not to come is finally here.'

'Do you want to....?' Sid gulped heavily and trailed off. Rohaan took a deep breath and nodded. He took the envelope, opened it and began reading.

11

Veera woke up very suddenly, which scared her. Her legs had yet again managed to tangle themselves with her sheets, resulting in her shivering. Not due to the fact that the AC was on, but the fact that she had just plunged into one of her nightmares again. There was a very odd thing about her nightmares: she didn't remember them at all. She always thoughts that this was good because it would be for the better only if she didn't remember those horrifying nightmares. The only nightmare she ever remembered was the one she had before the Royal Eureka sank, and she was hundred and one percent positive that she would remember it for the rest of her life. She had entered a state of deep shock for the past few days. They were still searching for her parents and a lot of other people as well.

Veera prayed daily that they be completely safe and sound. She also tried to console her heavy heart by thinking again and again that there might be a possibility that Sameera had managed to cling on to a lifeboat safely and was fine. However, a part of her heart, a deeply hidden part of her heart knew that Sameera had gone somewhere where even Veera could not call her back. But she herself didn't want this part to become a reality. Back to the present, Veera was sitting bolt upright in the single bed of her room. The room she had originally got was a one with twin beds. She had requested the authorities to change her room, as her heart ached every time she looked at the other bed. Her heart was beating loudly in her chest for God knows what reason. She had this bad feeling that something bad was bound to happen today. She slowly leaned back and rested her head on the soft pillow. She was staring up to the bland, white ceiling above her, but in reality, she wasn't seeing it at all.

Why did this happen to her of all people? The pain, the sense of betrayal, the feeling of being let down, was unbearable. Only a person who has truly lost any loved one can understand that feeling. She punched her pillow into a more comfortable position. She had lost count of how many times they (i.e. Sameera and her) had fought and she had called her beloved Di the worst sister in the entire world. But honestly, she was just the opposite. She was always a good sister, obedient daughter, true friend, studious student, athletic sportsperson and most important of all, a loyal human being. She always thought that she had got a much better sister then Sameera Di had. Tears soaked her pillow as soon as they began to pool down in her eyes and flow down her cheeks.

Recently, it had been a usual schedule. She cried herself to sleep and woke up with her pillow and neckline of shirt soaked with water. Veera was usually not a cry baby. Very rarely she would cry and such that it would soak her pillows: never. She turned to her side and grabbed her phone from the bedside cabinet. She checked the time: 7:53 a.m. She took two deep breaths and sat up. She wiped her eyes and blew her nose noisily, grabbed a random T-Shirt and jeans from her closet and headed towards the washroom. Twenty minutes later, she was standing in front of the mirror. She had smothered down her curls so that they didn't look like a rat's nest, but her eyes were rimmed red and looked rather watery and bloodshot. She briefly looked at her reflection, then grabbed some Kohl and applied it lightly. In such a situation and condition, she wouldn't have touched anything like that, but she was trying very hard to behave normally. She grabbed her wallet, phone and room keys and left, shutting the door behind her.

Veera sighed and glanced at her watch. 8:55 a.m. She had been sitting in the dining hall for the past forty minutes, waiting for Sid and Rohaan and was on her third cup of coffee. The SS Marina wasn't as lavish and luxurious as the Royal Eureka. It was fairly decent. For example, breakfast included muffins, toast, bread, and cheese, pork salad, chicken sausages, milk, coffee, tea, cocoa, sandwiches et cetera. Here it was just bread, milk, coffee, scrambled eggs and cereals.

The décor of the SS Marina's dining hall or any other café didn't give away a sense of euphoria or excitement. On the contrary, the grayish walls and yellow tables made the room appear rather dull and moody than it was actually. Time to go and see what they are doing, thought Veera as she pushed her cup away and got up.

She was standing in front of their room as she raised her hand and pushed the door hard. To her extreme surprise, the door opened. Either they are inside or they have gone somewhere and forgotten to lock the door, thought Veera as she stepped inside cautiously. 'Sid? Rohaan, are you there?' She called as she looked around. There was no one in the room. She checked the bathroom too, but it was also vacant. 'Where did they go and that too without informing. Ouch!' She had slipped on something on the ground and fallen with a thud. She sat up and found the envelope she had slipped on. 'What is…' Her hands had gone numb, her brain had shut down.

A tingling, painful sensation was spreading across her hands and legs, paralyzing them temporarily.

Conclusion of Search Report of Mr. and Mrs. Maheshwari.

'Oh no!' Cried out Veera, choking on her words as she hurriedly grabbed the dressing table's edge to hoist herself up. With the letter in one hand and the other shaking heavily, she sat down on one of the beds. No thought crossed her mind; no questions arose. When had Sid and Rohaan got this? Why did they not tell her? Have they already read this? None at all. Without wasting a single second, she fumbled out the piece of paper inside the envelope. It was not sealed, which meant its contents had already been read. She closed her eyes and took a deep breath before she started reading.

Dear Ms. Maheshwari,

As you may be aware that the Royal Eureka sank a few days ago, taking many innocent souls with it. A search was performed by the most expert of divers, to retain the dead bodies for the identification report. We have the results of the same. Mrs. Akshara Maheshwari, 38 Female, according to our reports, did manage to get on a lifeboat. However, due to unforeseen

circumstances, neither Mrs. Maheshwari nor the twenty-six people accompanying her on the lifeboat managed to reach the ship which was supposed to rescue them. We have identified her body, though it is now almost unrecognizable. Mr. Anant Maheshwari, 39 Male, didn't manage to get on a lifeboat and thus perished along with the ship. His body couldn't be found or identified.

The details on how to recover Mrs. Maheshwari's body will be sent to you shortly. If you wish, you may contact us using the telephone number or email id given below.

Our deepest condolences for your loss and hearty prayers for the departed souls,

The faculty/board members of the Royal Eureka

Veera didn't remember what happened after that. All she remembered was that the world had started spinning very fast for her all of a sudden, her knees felt weak and she just couldn't take it anymore. Her strength gave away and she collapsed. After that, everything went black.

***

Sid watched, full of exhaustion, as his brother circled the room worriedly, hands curled into fists and sweat glistening on his forehead. 'Bro, if you would have walked that much on a straight road, I swear you would have already reached Mumbai.' Said Sid. Rohaan looked over in his direction with a deep scowl embedded on his face. 'I am worried about two things right now. First, of course, Veera's health. She passed out in our room this morning. Second, is her reaction when she wakes up. You see...I didn't tell you before but I found the conclusion letter crumpled in her hand and the envelope inches away from her feet, just like someone had torn it off hurriedly. So, she has read that letter and that was the reason she fainted.' Said Rohaan, pursuing his lips. 'Are you kidding me?' Sid said, standing up. 'I wish I was. But it is true. Her entire family is now lost.' Said Rohaan. Sid was looking pitifully at the unconscious Veera in one of the beds in the infirmary when a nurse entered. 'Mr. Rohaan Parimal? You have a call.' She said, taking Veera's hand for checking her blood pressure. Rohaan nodded at Sid, gestured towards Veera with his eyes and left.

Rohaan instantly knew it was his mother's phone as he picked up the landline. He could hear the sounds of stifled sobs as pressed the receiver to his ears. His mom, Mrs. Surekha Suman was a headstrong woman who rarely cried. Rohaan instantly knew that she must be really shaken up. 'Hi, Mama. How are you? How is Baba?' He asked, trying to put the worry and tension for Veera out of his voice. His mom sobbed even harder.

'No, no. The question is how are you Rohaan? And Sid? My heart stopped beating when I learned that the ship had sunk. I tried calling you but...' 'Yeah, I know. While we were sitting in the lifeboat, my phone must have slipped from my pocket and fallen into the water. Sid had left his back in our room. Similarly, our luggage, clothes and other stuff were also left behind. We were given extras here.' Rohaan cut off his mother trying to divert the topic.

'How is Veera dear? And Sameera? Are they alright?' In just a second, Rohaan seemed to age fifty years. 'Veera is not fine, Mama. Sameera, aunty and uncle, all perished.' He said quietly. He heard his mother gasp and let out a cry of shock. About half a minute later, when she spoke, her voice wavered. 'That's shocking. I am feeling so bad and I didn't even know them properly. I just can't even imagine what Veera must be going through.' 'Yeah, I know.' Said Rohaan. Surekha was silent for a few minutes before she said, 'We've already made arrangements. Baba will go to Cape Town and pick you and Sid up.'

Rohaan wondered how to say what he wanted. None of Veera's relatives from Delhi had yet come forward and declared themselves to her. He had briefly considered asking Veera to tell their names and phone numbers to contact them but had then dropped the idea. 'Mama, you see…none of Veera's relatives have come forward yet to pick her up and take her to Delhi. So I was, you know, wondering if we could…'

His mom seemed to understand what he was trying to say, for she said sympathetically, 'Of course, my boy. You can get her too. I would absolutely love to have her in the house. I will talk to your Baba about it.'

Rohaan smiled and said 'Thank you. Speaking of which, can I speak to him? It has been about a week since I spoke to him last.' 'I am so sorry, my dear. He just left for office. But don't worry; I will make him speak to you as soon as possible. He was very worried. By the way, can I speak to Sid?' His mother asked. Rohaan called Sid outside, and he too spoke to their mother. Just as he had hung up, the same nurse came out and said 'The Miss is awake now. You can come inside and speak to her.' She left. Rohaan and Sid looked at each other. There was no escaping it now. The moment both of them had been dreading was here. With that, they both started walking towards the door; towards Veera.

12

'So, you must be Veera, the one my sons frequently told about on the phone, huh? Well, nice to meet you. Myself, Shekhar Parimal.'

Rohaan and Sid's Dad were a middle-aged man, with a few white strands added to his lush black hair, a light thin moustache and indeed a very pleasing and handsome smile. He currently had his hand outstretched towards Veera. She looked into his eyes and he found gloominess, pain and insecurity in her deep black eyes. Surekha told me about this girl, thought Mr. Parimal. She looks so lost. I wonder what it feels like to lose so many loved and dear ones at such a small and tender age.

Veera tried for a small smile, but it looked rather forced. 'The pleasure is all mine, sir. Thank you so much for agreeing to take me to Delhi. There wouldn't be many parents who would agree to take their kids' few weeks old friend to their home.' She said in a voice full of gratitude. Mr. Parimal waved his hand, saying it was no big deal. Veera's eyes met Rohaan's behind his Dad's shoulders and a smile crossed her face. He was dressed in a white T-Shirt, a pair of dark blue jeans and a black jacket.

His hair was a mess as usual. He looked cool in a I-Just-Rolled-Out-Of-Bed-And-I-Don't-Care-How-I-Look sort of way.

Sid meanwhile hadn't seen his father yet. He seemed to have forgotten his favorite shirt in his room and insisting that he couldn't afford to lose it, had gone inside again to retrieve it. Speaking of which, he had just come down the staircase hurriedly, holding his favorite 'I am the Coolest'. For the first time, he noticed his Dad standing there. Veera saw Mr. Parimal straighten and say in a tight, curt voice, 'Good morning Siddharth.' Sid's nostrils flared and Veera knew why. Sid hated his real name and the people who called him by it. There were only a few things that could exasperate him more than being addressed by 'Siddharth'. 'Hi, Dad.' Replied Sid as frostily. Veera couldn't understand why they were being so curt and frosty towards each other. As far as she knew Sid, he was a jovial person, who just didn't know how to handle anger or hatred. It was not his cup of tea to remain angry with someone for a long period of time.

'Why were Sid and Mr. Parimal being so hostile towards each other?' Asked Veera in a monotone voice to Rohaan as they made their way towards the car parking, with Sid walking behind them and

Mr. Parimal striding well ahead. 'I can't explain it, Veera. Sometimes, I myself don't understand it. It is just always that, Sid blames Baba for us being made to go and live in Southampton with our grandmother. Baba, meanwhile, thinks that Sid was the reason that we had to separate from him and Mama. Both are wrong, but each thinks that he is right.' Said Rohaan in a sad tone.

'At least Sid has a family to care about and a father to argue with. I don't even have that anymore.' Said Veera sadly.

Rohaan turned his face to look at her. She sighed, 'Sorry. It is just that, the past few weeks have been very difficult for me. I just can't seem to accept the fact that my family is gone. Lost forever.' She said, feeling a lump in her throat yet again which was threatening to burst. She might have shed more tears in the past two to three weeks than she ever had in her entire life put together. 'Hey-hey. It's OK. It's alright. To be honest, I didn't mind it. After everything that happened, I would have completely given up on life if I would have been in your place. The way you are coping with everything, with such a level of maturity, is incredible. Exemplary even.' Said Rohaan with a smile, trying to give confidence to Veera.

'What are you two talking about?' Asked Sid as he sped up to catch up with them, his brown rucksack slinging of his shoulder and a duffel bag in the other. 'Oh, nothing. Just, you know, random talking.' Said Veera turning around to look at him. Sid nodded, adjusting the bags on his shoulders to be comfortable. He looked as if his shoulders were aching too much from the weight of both the bags that he was carrying. This movement and look were not missed by Rohaan, who sighed and held out his hand. 'Here, give me one. Don't give me that look; I know well that your shoulders are throbbing.' He said.

Sid smiled gratefully and said 'Thanks Bro,' as he handed the rucksack to Rohaan and slipped the duffel into both his shoulders. Veera watched with a faint smile the affection and love and understanding between the two brothers. Sid may have a rocky relationship with his Dad and maybe even mom, but in the end, his brother is his strength, thought Veera fondly. She was reminded of Sameera and the kind of love and understanding they used to share. Di would always understand whatever I wanted without me saying anything, just like the way Rohaan does with Sid, thought Veera sadly. The thought of Sameera next reminded her of her mom and Dad as well. How Mumma used to scold me and how I used to hate it, but right now. Even that sounds endearing and lovable, she continued to think.

'Veera! Where are you going?' Shouted Rohaan behind her. She snapped out of her painful reverie and looked back. Lost in her thoughts, she had been walking even further away from the place where their cab stood. Mr. Parimal was gesturing her to come back while Rohaan was shouting to pull her out of her thoughts. Her cheeks turned red as she groaned, 'Coming, coming.' She muttered as she slowly began walking towards the cab. 'Penny for your thoughts?' Asked Sid as he opened the door to let Veera in. 'I don't have any to give you.' Replied Veera quietly as she slid inside. She, Rohaan and Sid were tightly wedged together in the backseat, owing to Sid's large and bulky duffel bag, which he had refused to keep in the luggage storage. Mr. Parimal was sitting in the passenger seat with the driver. As soon as they settled in, he turned towards them. 'All comfortable? You are having enough place to sit, Veera?'

The girl was back again in the tea stall. She had taken a seat at one of the benches again and was staring at her hands idly. Kesar thought this was a bit peculiar. She still hadn't answered his question. 'You want anything else, didi?'

Veera looked out of her seat's window as they landed in Delhi. The runway was cemented, but it was filled with colors of memories of each and every time Veera had come here. One time, three years ago, at Christmas. Then again on her twelfth birthday. The only difference this year was that there would be no suitcases full of memories to carry back to New York in the various compartments of her brain. There would be no Sameera Di to help her compile all the photographs into a rather ragged collage in their 'Sisters' Scrapbook'.

'Welcome to the Indira Gandhi International Airport of New Delhi. The temperature outside would be approximately 31 Degree Celsius. The checked-in luggage will be available at belt number three. We request you to remain seated in your seats until the seat belt sign is switched off. We thank you for choosing United Airways to fly with and hope you will choose us the next time as well.' A cool, clear female voice echoed through the chamber and jerked Sid open from his sleep, next to Veera. '

'We're already there?' He said groggily, looking left and right. 'No, man. We are still on the runway, waiting for the takeoff.' Said Rohaan, who was sitting beside Sid, sarcastically. Sid frowned at his elder brother while Veera gave a faint laugh.

Stereotypically, as soon as the plane slowed its speed, almost all the passengers got up and hurriedly started taking out their carry bags from their overhead cabins. Mr. Parimal, who was sitting a seat behind them to the right, came over to their seats.

'Had an enjoyable flight, kiddos? All right, so, Veera, Surekha had a talk with your aunt and uncle. They are currently in Shimla. They had gone holidaying about a week ago and they are devastated to know about…the situation. They insisted on coming back right away, but we told them that it would be fine for us to keep you with us for the next four days. Are you OK with that, my dear?' He said, mainly talking with Veera.

'Of course, she is. Could that be any more obvious?' Sid said dismissively. Mr. Parimal turned towards Sid with a horribly fake smile on his face. 'Whenever I would be talking with Veera or any other person for that matter, you will not interrupt. Am I clear, Siddharth?' He said with a dangerous edge to his voice. Rohaan, just like Veera, seemed to find the situation in dangerous waters and decided to steer it away from them. 'Baba, I've already had a talk with Veera regarding this and she is OK with that.' Said Rohaan, clearing his throat.

That was the end of the conversation.

Mrs. Surekha Parimal was looking like a recipient of Mrs. India when Veera first met her. Long and lush black hair tied back in a neat plait with a golden rubber band, a prim and proper line of kohl covering her kind and benevolent eyes which were precisely the same shade as Sid and Rohaan. A Bengali white red saari with light gold earrings and a necklace.

She enveloped both Sid and Rohaan in her arms as soon as they saw her at the arrival gate. She had shed a few tears and asked her husband about the journey etcetera when finally she spotted a very nervous Veera standing behind Mr. Parimal. She hadn't even let her say the lines she had been practicing and had instead hugged Veera, as tightly she had done with her two sons. 'Veera, I am feeling so happy to meet you finally after weeks of hearing of Veera this and Veera that from Rohaan and Sid.' She said, after releasing her tight hold on Veera. She planted a kiss on Veera's forehead and stepped away, eyeing her appreciatively. After the introductions by Sid, the four of them settled themselves in Parimal's Innova and made their way towards the Parimal house.

The Parimal house was a three-bedroom house in Vasant Kunj, New Delhi. The living room was spacious, full of light and white curtains. A photograph of Sid and Rohaan stood on the center table, along with a tea kettle and a few teacups. 'Muniya! They are here! Quickly get the snacks and drinks.' Called Mrs. Parimal as the children deposited their backpacks along with the sofa. She turned a blind eye to all of Veera's protests about such treatment and insisted on providing the hospitality.

The Parimals' housemaid, Muniya, was a lady in her thirties, with rather large front teeth and a creaky voice. She welcomed them with blessings for Veera and a kiss on the forehead each for Sid and Rohaan. As she watched Sid and Rohaan bickering sweetly, Veera realized that somewhere, sometime, they both had become family to her.

13

Veera's aunt and uncle were unsure about whether they should smile or not when they saw Veera enter the living room, followed by Sid and Rohaan. She stepped forward and hugged her aunt, who started sobbing. 'Oh –hic- my Veera – hic.' She repeatedly said as she stroked Veera's hair and choked, trying to control her tears. 'Don't, aunt. How are Shreya and Sunaina?' Asked Veera. Both Shreya and Sunaina were the twin thirteen-year-old sisters of Veera. 'They are alright, but that is not the point.'

Veera's uncle planted a kiss on Veera's forehead and turned to Mr. Parimal and Mrs. Parimal. 'Thank you so much for taking care of our Veera. We could have come earlier but could not.' Mr. Parimal waved away their apologies and took Veera aside to talk separately. 'Veera, in these four days that you have spent with us, you have become family. It feels just like we already have a very special bonding with you, which is really close to Surekha's, Rohaan's Siddharth's and my heart. Though we have known you for about six weeks, it feels like we have known you for years. So, all I want to say is that whenever and wherever you need any of the Parimal family, we will be there for you. 'I assure and guarantee you that.' He said sincerely. Veera's eyes started to get watery and she gave a thankful and grateful smile to Mr. Parimal; wordlessly thanking him for giving her such a great family. Next, she went to Sid and Rohaan. 'Good thing you are staying close to us, we can come and visit you sometimes.' Said Sid.

'Take care, V. 'Will miss your morning wake up call.' said Rohaan. Veera just nodded, not trusting herself to speak. She stepped forward, holding out her arms and blinking back tears. Both the boys stepped forward and they shared a trio-hug. After what seemed like one or two minutes, they separated and Veera suspected she saw Sid wiping his eyes and Rohaan's eyes watering abnormally.

'Thank you, guys. I really needed that,' choked out Veera. God, why was she becoming so emotional? It's not like she is leaving them forever, is she? Somehow, she just couldn't shake off the feeling of dread as she stepped out of Parimal household.

'This is *amazing.*'

****

Sid devoured the ice scream smoothie like it was the best thing in the entire world and he had been in a period of starvation for centurions. His entire face was splattered with the vanilla essence and whipped cream and Hershey's Chocolate Syrup. Veera, who was sitting beside him, looked around to see the table beside them. All the six occupants—two kids and four adults were glaring at Sid with disgust. All of them were clutching knives and forks and had napkins pinned around their throats tightly, that Veera was sure that they must be suffocating for sure. She turned towards Sid, who had already finished his smoothie, and was staring longingly at the empty glass. Deciding that nothing could ever change him, she turned towards her other best friend.

'So you are attending Delhi University then?' She asked Rohaan. 'Yeah. The session starts this fall. What about you?' He replied, fiddling with his smoothie spoon. 'Oh, I have already decided. I am gonna attend an all year, all girls boarding school. Which one, I am yet to decide.' She said. 'Guys! Can we please not talk about depressing stuff today? You are ruining my good and jolly mood!' Moaned Sid, throwing up his hands over his head dramatically. 'Shut up, drama queen. What are you going to do?' Said Veera, slapping him on his arm.

'I think I am going to…wait, did you call Sid Parimal a drama queen?' He said, looking horrified. Veera and Rohaan glanced at each other and burst out laughing. 'I think I am going to be a dropout this year.' Veera and Rohaan stopped laughing and turned to look at Sid, their mouths hanging open. 'I think I misheard you, Sid. Can you please repeat what you said?' Said Rohaan nervously. Sid sighed and said 'No, you heard me right, Bro. I want to be a dropout this year. I want to pursue my dream of becoming a rock star.'

'You gotta be kidding me! Why do you want to abandon your education for becoming a rock star? This is idiocy!' Shouted Rohaan, standing up. 'Rohaan!' Whispered Veera, tugging his jacket's sleeve. 'This is not the place. You are creating a scene. Can we please go outside and talk?'

Rohaan seemed to find sense in her words, for he fished out a couple of bills from his pocket and threw them on the table. He stomped out of the café and a nervous Veera and scared Sid followed suit. They found him standing in the park right outside the café. 'Please justify your childish and immature behavior.' Rohaan spat at Sid. 'Bro, please just hear me out, OK? You know how passionate I am about becoming a rock star, right? Right. You of all people know that pretty well. And I just don't want to study this year, because I want to enroll myself in bands and start like a professional. And if I go to school this year, it would be a real burden on me.

Moreover, you only used to say that I have the potential of becoming a full time, famous rock star. I am requesting you, Bro. I can't do this without your or Veera's support. You agree with me, Veera?' He said, looking directly at Veera at his last words. Sid just had this pleading look in his eyes that Veera just couldn't tear her mind away from. She had never seen him looking so vulnerable. But on the other side, there was Rohaan, who would never want anything bad happening to his dear brother. Who to support in this matter?

Finally, she said, 'Sid, I understand your dreams and emotions well and trust me, you have my full support there. But…' she looked at Sid and Rohaan who was protesting silently. 'But I think that leaving or abandoning your education just for the sake of it is not totally right. You are not even an adult. I would just say that this is a very crucial point in your life, where you find two different roads, you need to choose from. It is entirely up to you, but I'd say, choose wisely.'

Sid nodded enthusiastically, for he already had a response ready to that. 'I know. I have already read a few online programs and brochures. They offer a complete improvising voice class, for a fee of course. I have to pass a kind of aptitude test to get admission in that class. After I graduate from there, I can join any band for practice. Another option is part-time YouTubing.

Creating online videos to get enough subscriptions as funds. It is my dream guys.' He seemed so excited, like a five-year-old promise a huge slab of chocolate. 'Sorry to interrupt, but I have another query. What about Mama and Baba? How distressed will they be when they find out their younger son wants to be a dropout in the most professionally crucial stage of his life? Has anyone even given a damn about it? Baba wants you to become an Engineer. Though he is a bit hostile towards you, at heart, there is nothing more he wishes then seeing you being successful and happy. Have you any idea how much he loves you? Probably more than any other valuable thing in this entire universe. And you want to break and shatter all his dreams like an effing castle of cards? That is bloody selfish of you, Sid!' Shouted Rohaan, his voice cracking under the strain of all the emotions; anger, love, respect fear etcetera-etcetera.

'Bro, I am sorry. I know how big a shock I will give to both of them, but I…just can't help it. I know how sad and upset and frustrated they would be, but you think that they won't be happy when they see their son, their Sid happy and successful in his career?' Questioned Sid weakly, trying to approach Rohaan with his hand but he slapped his hand away, refusing to look in his younger brother's eyes.

'But that is the root cause of the problem, isn't it? It is so difficult to be world-famous and...I don't know! If you are one in a million, then only you'll be 'happy and successful'!' Said Rohaan. Time to break the fight up thought Veera. 'OK-OK, guys, seriously, this is becoming too much. Let's just, you know, sit and talk? I know, it will resolve the issue easily. Come on, guys! You are almost adults, please behave like one.' She said, stepping between both the boys. Both of them looked away and when Veera glared at both, they nodded (in Sid's case) and shrugged (in Rohaan's case) with obvious hesitation and reluctance.

'I want to go home.' Said Rohaan curtly, before Veera could propose what they should do next, though admittedly, she couldn't think of any plans or proposals at the current moment. Before either Veera or Sid could say anything, he stormed off, hired a cab and left. 'I have spoiled everything, right?' Asked Sid, taking a seat on one of the many benches in the park and taking his head in his hands. He ruffled his hair and rubbed his eyes wearily. Veera took a seat next to Sid and kept a hand on his shoulder.

'Listen to me, Sid. You did not spoil anything. Dreaming or speaking about your dreams is not bad. On the contrary, it is the birthright of anyone and everyone. But the way you handled the situation, I would say that it could have been handled in a better and more mature manner. Things like this take time and patience, they do not happen in a course of one minute. You need to give time to Rohaan to accept it. I am sure that someday, sometime, he will.' She said. His face still in his hands, he mumbled between his fingers. 'What if he does not?'

Veera sighed before replying. 'I am hundred and one percent sure he would get it. He is your brother and he will want only the best in the entire world for you. I have seen how much he loves you and how much he is concerned about you. As I said, a decision of entire life cannot be taken in a few minutes, right? The same goes for acceptance by family as well.'

'Family. I am scared of Mama and Baba's reaction. I know that I don't like Baba that much, but still, I do care about his reaction and thoughts regarding me.'

'That can only happen when, as I said earlier, you remain calm. I am sure that they will understand, Sid. They are your parents after all. They will only want the best for you, same as Rohaan.'

'Guess you are right. I will just have to deal with it.'

'Exactly.' A moment of silence and understanding between both the best friends. 'Come on, Sid! You are being depressed yourself and that is now making me depressed as well!' She said, tugging his arm in an effort to pull it away from his face. 'OK-OK, fine.' He removed his palms from the front of his face and stood up. When he turned to look at her, she could see the old Sid's twinkle in his eyes, though it was concealed by a layer of worry and sadness. 'Come on, I am going to drop you home and then jog to my house from there.' Veera nodded and he went to the taxi stand to hire a cab.

***

'Hi, Veera Di.' Shreya popped her head inside Veera's bedroom. 'Mom's saying that dinner will be ready in fifteen minutes.' She said. 'OK. Come, sit.' She said, patting the place on the bed next to her. Shreya smiles and came in, closing the door behind her. 'Where is Sunaina? She was not at home when I came.' Said Veera.

'Oh, she is at her basketball practice. They are having a championship in about a week's time so she is out till late practicing.' She said. Though they were twins, they could not be any more different. While Sunaina was more outdoorsy, Shreya preferred to have a book in hand other than a football or basketball. Sunaina was outspoken and an extrovert; she liked to speak her heart out and was not afraid of giving anybody, anytime a piece of her mind. Shreya was an introvert and was rather quiet and shy with strangers. Though being so different in nature, both the girls rubbed in as comfortably. The only way of distinguishing Sunaina from Shreya was by the red mark over her left eye; a mark gained when she was playing rugby a few years ago.

Veera and Shreya had just been talking for a few minutes when suddenly they heard a door slam and a grumble which sounded unmistakably like Sunaina. 'She's back.' Said Shreya, getting up and gesturing Veera to come along. 'You go on, I will come after tidying my room a bit.'

When Veera entered the living room, she saw Sunaina lying on the couch. She had her foot in Veera's aunt's lap, who was applying an ice pack to her daughter's swollen ankle. 'What happened?' She asked, taking a seat next to Sunaina. 'Hi, Veera Di. Oh, nothing much. I just fell down while coming back. Landed on the wrong foot and ended up twisting it.' She said. But she did wince when Veera's aunt applied the ice pack to the most swollen part of her ankle's joint. 'Nothing much? God knows where your mind was and how were you walking that you ended up twisting your ankle! This girl and her antics.' Scolded Veera's aunt. 'You will not move until I come back with another ice pack.'

She slowly got up and carefully put Sunaina's ankle on the couch. Sunaina rolled her eyes and said 'Mom, I am fine.' 'I can see how fine you are!' Huffed Veera's aunt. As she was going towards the kitchen, she turned back. 'And I am going to call Coach to tell him that you will not be able to attend tomorrow morning's practice due to an injury.' She said. Sunaina looked outraged. 'Mom, no way...'

'Either that or I call up and tell him that you will not be able to attend any of the championship matches. You decide.'

Mom, you can't do this.'

'I assure you, I can. Don't forget I have not signed the consent form yet. Decide.'

'Mom.'

'Decide.'

'But...'

'No championship for you then.'

Shreya and Veera were watching the latter's aunt and Sunaina arguing like an interesting tennis match between Rafael Nadal and Roger Federer.

'That is so unfair.'

'Shreya, hand me the phone.'

Sunaina huffed and sent her mother the best glare she could muster. 'Fine. Do as you please.' She said. Veera's aunt smirked victoriously as she went into the kitchen. Shreya kept a hand on Sunaina's shoulder with mock understanding. 'Oh, shut up.' Grumbled Sunaina.

Dinner that night was Chicken Gravy and Rice. 'Hmmm! This is really good, mom!' Said Shreya, moaning in appreciation. Her mother smiled. 'Flatterer.' She said swatting Shreya's arm. 'Pass me the curry, Veera. Thanks.' Said Veera's uncle, extending his hand. Veera did, and she had just put a bite of rice in her mouth when her uncle spoke again. 'So, have you decided which boarding school you want to attend? Because we need to start the admission process.'

Veera swallowed and spoke. 'Yes, actually I have been considering a few options. There is The Sindhiya Kanya School in Gwalior or the Welham High School in Dehradun. Even the Mayo College Girls School would do.'

'So you are still sticking up with your decision of attending an all-girls boarding school?' Asked Veera's aunt, looking skeptical. Veera nodded. 'I don't know why the prospect attracts me so much, but I just want to.'

'I will find out the admission processes of all the three schools tomorrow. We will apply for all three and then on the basis of admission and choice, you can decide which one you want.'

The discussion ended then and there.

Next afternoon, Veera was sitting on the Parimal's sofa, reading a book. Sid sitting on the floor and leaning across Veera's legs as he played his all-time favorite Clash of Clans on his mobile phone. Rohaan was sitting on the armchair, as he read the Sunday supplementary magazine. The tension between both the brothers had decreased drastically.

'Hey! Listen to this article! It is about a flower that blooms once in twelve years!' Cried out Rohaan. 'One in twelve years? Blimey!' Said Sid, looking up from his phone. 'Read it aloud!' Said Veera enthusiastically. *'Strobilanthes kunthiana or NeelaKurinji is a once in twelve year's scene to view in the picturesque setting of Munnar in the Western Ghats of Southern India. Kurinji earned the Nilgiri Mountains its name, which means blue, typically the same as the rare purplish-blue flower. Its season shall start in October 2018 and end in Mid December the same year.'* He read out aloud.

'Stobi-what?' Said Sid, looking clueless as usual. 'Strobilanthes kunthiana.' Said, Rohaan reading up it from the magazine. 'Twelve years! That's a long period.' Said Veera, looking surprised. 'And from what is written in the continuation of the article, they are really beautiful to view.' Said Rohaan, eyes still glued to the magazine. 'They would be so cool to visit.' Said Sid dreamily. Then, like a magnet both the brothers looked at each other and started grinning maniacally like they understood what the other was thinking. 'What are you so excited about?' Asked Veera looking at them. 'A trip to Munnar which includes Rohaan and Sid Parimal and Veera Maheshwari!' They shouted together.

Epilogue

Sid, Veera and Rohaan were sitting in front of Mr. and Mrs. Parimal. The air in their living room was tense. The three of them had just laid out their plan of a three-day trip to Munnar. Mr. Parimal was sitting, brow furrowed and arms crossed. He seemed to be listing all the pros and cons of sending one just-adult and two almost-but-not-adults to a leisure trip. 'Baba, please, we really want to go on this trip. You see, I will be gone to Delhi University and Veera will be gone to Sindhiya Kanya. And Sid, well, he...' at this, Rohaan threw a furtive glance at Sid. 'He will be gone to-to whichever school he fancies.'

'Can I talk to Rohaan and Siddharth for a minute?' Asked Mr. Parimal to Veera. When she nodded, he added 'Alone?'

The details were blurry on what happened next, but all she knew was that the next moment, she was standing in front of their hotel, with Sid on her right and Rohaan on Sid's right, each carrying a backpack on their shoulder. 'This place looks good. I sincerely hope that the food is equally good.' Said Sid, as usual, rubbing his stomach in anticipation. All three of them quickly checked into their respective rooms and headed towards the hotel restaurant to have dinner only because all the other restaurants would have already closed due to the fact that it was about 11:30 at night.

Veera got up at 5:00 a.m. Not being able to sleep anymore, she got up and brushed her teeth and after taking a hot water shower, changed into a red polka dot dress. She also grabbed a blue jacket in case it was cold outside and stepped out of her room. The sun had not completely risen yet, but there was a bit of light. As their hotel was just beside the Neela Kurinji hills, she slowly went up a small hillside. It was filled with greenery. Flowers of various colors were blossoming here and there, and there were a few people taking a stroll or doing Yoga. After roaming here and there and thinking about meaningless things, she spotted a tea stall at a distance. A young boy was standing there, observing his surroundings. She slowly made her way towards the tea stall.

'Didi!' Kesar's voice rang out, bringing her out of reverie. 'Those boys there are motioning you to go over to them.' He said pointing towards the narrow hillside. Sid and Rohaan were standing there and waving their hands to catch her attention.

She glanced at the time in her watch. 6:32 a.m. She groaned mentally. God, how long had she sat there, thinking about her past and looking like a complete idiot? She slowly trudged her way towards them. 'Good morning. Want to go and get breakfast?' asked Rohaan. She nodded and just as they were walking away, the sun rose completely. As the sun-rays touched the ground, she looked over her shoulder and saw something she hadn't seen before. The valley beside the mountains was filled with a sea of purplish-blue. The flowers blossomed completely, forming a saga of golden and blue. It was a splendid sight, watching the flowers become beautiful to their fullest, sparkling with a sense of joy, that yes, it is a new day. A new beginning. End of the previous day, previous faults. 'What are you looking at?' Came Sid's voice behind her, as well as a hand on her shoulder which was surely Rohaan's.

Just as the sun rays marked a new day in everyone's lives, it marked a new beginning in her life as well. She turned away and smiled to herself. 'Nothing,' she whispered, only for the word to be blown away with the wind. She followed both her best friends down the mountains. Just as she was about to step down, she thought she caught a glimpse of Sameera Di, her mom and her Dad smiling down upon her but when she looked back the second time, they were gone. From the mountains of Munnar, from the ground of this Earth, but certainly not from her memories.

Is this the beginning of the end?

******************The End******************

My Dear Reader,

My sincere and heartfelt gratitude for choosing to read my second book in the form of a Novel. I hope you enjoy my fictional style of writing.

Your review, opinion and feedback matters to me at a very high rate.

I can be reached at

email: anantineemishra07@gmail.com

Instagram: anantineejhumpamishra.

Best,

AM